GLORY O'BRIEN'S
HISTORY
OF THE
FUTURE

GLORY O'BRIEN'S
HISTORY
OF THE
FUT

URE

A NOVEL BY

A.S. KING

Ⓛ Ⓑ

LITTLE, BROWN AND COMPANY

NEW YORK ◆ BOSTON

Little, Brown and Company

Hachette Book Group
1290 Avenue of the Americas, New York, NY 10019
Visit our website at lb-teens.com

Little, Brown and Company is a division of Hachette Book Group, Inc.
The Little, Brown name and logo are trademarks of Hachette Book Group, Inc.

The publisher is not responsible for websites (or their content) that are not owned by the publisher.

First Edition: October 2014

Library of Congress Cataloging-in-Publication Data

King, A. S. (Amy Sarig), 1970–
Glory O'Brien's history of the future : a novel / by A.S. King. — First edition.
pages cm
Summary: "As her high school graduation draws near, Glory O'Brien begins having powerful and terrifying visions of the future as she struggles with her long-buried grief over her mother's suicide"— Provided by publisher.
ISBN 978-0-316-22272-3 (hardcover) — ISBN 978-0-316-22274-7 (ebook) — ISBN 978-0-316-36457-7 (library edition ebook) [1. Clairvoyance—Fiction. 2. Best friends—Fiction. 3. Friendship—Fiction. 4. Fathers and daughters—Fiction. 5. Photography—Fiction. 6. Suicide—Fiction. 7. Eccentrics and eccentricities—Fiction.] I. Title.
PZ7.K5693Glo 2014 [Fic]—dc23 2013041670

10 9 8 7 6 5 4 3 2 1

RRD-C

Printed in the United States of America

For my girls

The future is no more uncertain than the present.

—Walt Whitman

PROLOGUE

The clan of the petrified bat

So we drank it—the two of us. Ellie drank it first and acted like it tasted good. I followed. And it wasn't half bad.

When we woke up the next morning, everything was different. We could see the future. We could see the past. We could see *everything*.

You might say, "Why did you drink a bat?" Or, "How did you drink a bat?" Or, "Who would do something like that?"

But we weren't thinking about it at the time. It's like being on a fast train that crashes and someone asking you why you didn't jump before it crashed.

You wouldn't jump because you *couldn't* jump. It was going too fast.

And you didn't know the crash was coming, so why would you?

BOOK ONE

The origin of everything

School is the same as anything else. You do it because you're told to do it when you're little enough to listen. You continue because someone told you it was important. It's like you're a train in a tunnel. Graduation is the light at the end.

Hippie weirdo freaks

Ellie Heffner told me that the day she graduated would be the day she left her family and ran away forever. She'd been telling me that since we were fifteen years old.

"They're freaks," she said. "Hippie weirdo freaks."

I couldn't argue with her. She did live with hippie weirdo freaks.

"Will you come back and visit me, at least?" I asked.

She looked at me, disappointed. "You won't still be here then, will you?"

I had one week to go. Three more school days: Monday, Tuesday, Wednesday, and optional Baccalaureate on Friday and then a weekend wait to graduate on Monday. I still got postcards and letters from colleges and universities in the mail every week. I still threw each of them away without opening them.

It was Sunday night and Ellie and I were sitting on the steps on my front porch facing her house, which was across the road.

"I don't know," I answered. "I have no idea where I'll be."

I couldn't tell her the truth about where I thought I'd be. I almost did a few times, weak times when I was gripped by fear. I'd almost told her everything. But Ellie was...Ellie. Ever since we were little, she'd change the rules of a game halfway through.

You don't tell your biggest secrets to someone like that, right?

Anyway. I had a week until I graduated. I had zero plans, zero options, zero friends.

But I didn't tell Ellie that either because she thought she was my best friend.

It was complicated.

It had always been complicated.

It would always be complicated.

The origin of the bat

The bat lived at Ellie's house. We saw it first on a weekend that February. She pointed at the tiny lump of fur lodged in the corner of the back porch and said, "Look. A hibernating bat."

We saw it again in March and it hadn't moved. We talked about the bat's upcoming awakening and how it would soon swoop to the surface of Ellie's pond and eat newly hatched insects and touch its tiny wingtips off the water.

But spring came and the bat didn't move. Didn't swoop. Didn't seem to be dining on any of the tasty neighborhood pond bugs. One of its elbows—if that's what bats have—stuck out a little, like it was broken or something. We talked about how it might have an injury or a birth defect.

"Like the way I can't bend this finger down all the way since I broke it," Ellie said, showing me her right-hand index finger.

Life on Ellie's commune was different. They used hammers before they could walk. They didn't have any plastic. They swung on a homemade swing with a wooden plank as a seat. They played on the frozen pond without adult supervision and had chores that involved livestock. Ellie was in charge of chickens. One time when she was seven, she broke her finger while hammering a door hinge on a chicken house back into place.

I was convinced that the bat was out of hibernation and was simply nesting there at night in the exact same place under the eaves of her back porch. If we were in any way smart, we'd have stayed until dusk that night to watch the bat leave in order to answer our curiosities about it, but we didn't. Ellie had commune chores and a secret boyfriend. I had reluctant homework and senioritis. We were happy believing the bat was fine.

When we met on Easter Monday in late April, the bat was still there, elbow pointed to the eastern horizon like it had been since winter. Ellie found a stick and poked it and then sniffed the stick.

"Doesn't stink," she said. "And there are no flies or anything."

"Don't bats have fleas?" I asked. "I heard they carry fleas and ticks and stuff."

"I think it's dead," Ellie said.

"Doesn't look dead," I said.

"Doesn't look alive, either," Ellie said.

She poked it again and it didn't move. Then she nudged

the stick up into the siding where she could force the whole bat out with one slice and it fell into her mother's sprouting summer lilies. Ellie reached into the lime-green and came out with this oddity—perfectly intact, still furry, still with eyeballs, still with paper-thin wings folded like it was resting.

We leaned down and looked at it.

"It's petrified?" Ellie said.

"Probably more like mummified," I said.

She ignored my correction and placed the bat on the picnic table and went into the house and got a jar. I took a picture of the jar. I named the picture in my head. *Empty Jar.*

"It's so light," Ellie said, weighing the bat in her palm. "Do you want to hold it before I put it in?"

I put my hands out and she placed it in my palm and we looked at it. Even though it was dead, Ellie seemed to see it as a new stray pet that needed a mother or something. When I put it in the jar, she sealed the lid and held it up and said, "I christen thee the petrified bat! Hear ye, hear ye, the petrified bat is king!"

"Might be a queen," I said.

"Whatever," Ellie said. She inspected it through the glass. "It's alive and dead at the same time or something."

"Yeah."

"It's the closest I've ever come to God," Ellie said.

"Amen." I was being sarcastic. Because Ellie said stuff like that sometimes and it was annoying. Because we were seventeen and this was silly, us finding a bat and acting like it was something special. This was what nine-year-olds did.

But then something serious came over me. I said, "Hold on. Let me see it." Ellie handed the jar to me and as I looked at it—a tiny lump of mummified fur—I said, "Maybe it *is* God."

The bat was dead but somehow it represented life because it looked alive. It was mysterious and obvious in one hollow, featherweight package.

"We'll put it in the shed," Ellie said. "My mom will never find it there because that's where we keep the cleaning supplies."

Ellie's mother didn't believe in cleaning.

My mother was dead, and I had no idea if she was ever a clean freak or what.

The ballad of Darla O'Brien

My mother wasn't conveniently dead, like in so many stories about children, whether they jarred dead bats or were attracted to beasts in woodland castles. She didn't die to help me overcome some obstacle by myself or to make me a more sympathetic character.

She haunted me—and not in some run-of-the-mill Hollywood way. There were no floating bedsheets or chains clanking in the night as I tiptoed to the bathroom to pee.

My mother, Darla O'Brien, was a photographer. She haunted the walls of our house with pictures. She was always there and never there. We could never see her, but every day, I saw her pictures. She was a great photographer, but she never became famous because we didn't live in New York City. Or that's what I've heard she said.

Getting dead didn't make her famous either.

Regardless, having a dead mother isn't convenient, especially when she died because she stuck her head in an oven and turned on the gas.

That is not convenient.

Although, I'd argue that there is some convenience in having a death machine right there in your kitchen waiting for the moment you finally get the nerve to do it. I'd argue that's more convenient than a fast-food drive-thru. You don't even have to leave your house to stick your head in the oven.

You don't even have to change out of your bathrobe.

You don't even have to take your kid to preschool where it was Letter *N* Day and she was ready to show off her acorn collection. You don't have to remember to do anything but breathe in and breathe out.

That's about as convenient as it gets.

What's inconvenient is: Living in a world where no one wants to talk to you about your dead mother because it makes them uncomfortable.

What's inconvenient is: Not having a mother at middle school graduation. Not having a mother when I tried to figure out how to shave under my arms. Not having a mother when I got my period. My dad was helpful; but he's a feminist, not an actual woman.

I always knew that one day, it would be inconvenient as hell not having a mother at high school graduation. The last few weeks of senior year were filled with all the girls in my homeroom talking about buying dresses and shoes and all I could think about was how small those things seemed.

I sat in homeroom thinking *Shoes. Dresses. Disposable bullshit.*

I sat in homeroom thinking *Where am I really going, anyway?*

Though my yearbook photographer duties were over because the year's book was done, I still carried my camera with me everywhere. I took candid shots of those girls talking about their dresses and shoes. I took pictures of my teachers trying to teach near-empty classrooms. I took pictures of the people who thought they were my friends, but who I'd never let all the way in.

I didn't let anyone sign my yearbook. I decided: Why fake it?

Everything tasted like radiation

Ellie hadn't been to public school with me since we finished the eighth grade, and in the four years since, she'd said, "Homeschooling is faster because there's no repeating everything all the time," about eleven trillion times to me. Maybe it was true. Maybe not. Seemed to me homeschooling was just another way to keep all those kids in the commune from seeing the real world.

I didn't like the real world, but I was glad I knew about it.

Darla O'Brien didn't like the real world either, so she stuck her head in an oven.

My dad loved the real world. He ate it up. Literally. He weighed two hundred and forty pounds now. Not a bad weight unless you were five foot four and 120 pounds when you started out.

Dad had never replaced the oven. Not even with an electric one. Our kitchen had never had an oven since Letter *N* Day. Just a freezer full of food that could be cooked by the microwave.

Everything tasted like radiation.

Ellie wouldn't come to my house if we were cooking because she believed microwaves gave you cancer. She never could understand why we didn't have a huge stove like they had on the commune—a stove that could pickle and blanch and reduce fruit into jam for the winter.

"It's not like that could happen twice, right?" she'd said once. By *that*, she meant Darla sticking her head in the oven.

I'd answered, "No. No, I guess that couldn't happen twice."

But it could. Right? There were still two people left in my house. I was one of them. Whenever I thought about what Ellie had said, my guts churned. Sometimes I got diarrhea from it. Sometimes I threw up. It wasn't as easy as *it can't happen twice*. Anyone who knew anything about what Darla did knew it sometimes *did* happen twice because it's often hereditary. But Ellie just said things without thinking. That was hereditary too.

Ellie's mother, Jasmine Blue Heffner, believed that the microwave oven was no different from an atomic bomb because it was invented by defense contractors during World War II.

I figured by the time Ellie applied to colleges, she'd either be smarter than me from learning *so much faster* in homeschool, or she'd be so brainwashed by Jasmine Blue that she would score badly on her SAT because she believed a microwave oven was the same as an atomic bomb.

Ellie might have defended homeschooling to me, but deep down she knew what she was missing. From the day she stopped getting on the yellow school bus with me she started complaining about the commune. It was as if school was her one real-world connection, and cutting it off made her feel like a bird in a cage.

She asked about what other girls were wearing to school. She asked about makeup. She asked about boys, TV shows, social media sites, dances, sports games.

Mostly, she asked about sex, even though we'd just turned fourteen.

"Did you have health class today?" she'd asked.

"Yeah."

"Did you get the rubber demonstration yet?"

"Today we learned about meth," I'd said.

I told her that real sex ed wasn't until eleventh grade and she looked disappointed. "I think that's too late to learn about sex."

"Yeah. By then, we know everything already," I'd said.

We knew enough. I had the Internet at home. (Ellie did not have the Internet. Jasmine Blue believed the Internet was an atomic bomb full of porn and lies. In that order.) By fifth grade, we'd Googled it. First we Googled *penis*. We looked for images. That was the day we found the butter penis. A penis carved from butter—anatomically correct. We made jokes about it. *What good is that if it melts? Bet it tastes better than the real thing.* We wondered why anyone would sculpt a penis out of butter. But then we found penis cakes, penis candy molds and penis lollipops, and we figured adults were gross.

That's as far as it went in fifth grade. Adults are gross. Nothing more to it.

We made a promise that day. We promised to tell each other the minute we had sex. Both of us doubted in fifth grade that it would ever happen, but if it did, we swore we would tell each other and talk about it.

In middle school, before homeschooling, Ellie became an expert, as if she was preparing for the most important event of her life. She got her friends to buy her the latest women's magazines and she'd talk about orgasms and balls and *how to please your man*. She would sometimes give the magazines to me to keep for her. I had a box of her contraband under my bed. Mostly magazines and eye shadow. A condom that a random boy gave to her. A weekend section of the newspaper with a page of exotic dancers, with names like *Leather Love, Lacey Snow, Shy-Anne*, who would perform at the local lap dancing bars. I looked through the magazines sometimes, too. In front of Ellie I pretended I wasn't interested. But I was.

In front of everyone else, I pretended I didn't care about all the stuff girls start to care about in middle school—the right clothes, shoes, mascara, hair products, sex—but I did. I was interested in the *why. Why? Why do we care so much about this?*

I wasn't sure why I cared about not caring. Or why I didn't care about not caring.

I figured it had something to do with what everyone else was avoiding talking about, which was Darla. Maybe had Darla still been around, she'd have given me a direction. Or something.

Jasmine Blue's homeschool sex education was contained in a simple mantra. *If you do it too early, you'll regret it.* I watched as each mention made Ellie more curious and more rebellious and more determined to have sex just because she wanted to test Jasmine's theory.

"What do you think it's like?" she would ask me, even though she knew it made me uncomfortable to talk about it. I think she figured since she was fourteen and curious, so was I.

"I don't know," I'd say. "I don't really care."

"You don't *care*? Really? Come on. You care."

I didn't care.

"What about that kid on the bus you used to crush on? Didn't you ever think about doing it with him?" she asked.

"Markus Glenn?"

"Yeah."

"Don't you remember? He was such a perv."

She picked at a fingernail that was bothering her. "What'd he do again?"

"The porn guy."

"Ohhh. Yeah. Him," she said. "So, who do you like now?"

"Nobody."

I never told her that after Markus Glenn showed me those pictures on his computer in seventh grade, he asked me to touch him there where his shorts were sticking up like a tipi. When I wouldn't touch it and I told him I was going home, he said, "You're never going to be a real woman acting like that, you know! Anyway, you're flat as a board!"

16

I didn't tell her that from that moment forward, I never even wanted breasts because then kids like Markus Glenn would look at them. I didn't tell her that from that moment on, I sometimes didn't know what a woman was really supposed to look like.

"You liked one kid in your whole life? I don't buy it."

"I told you. I don't care," I'd said.

I picked up my camera and held it at arm's length and took a picture of myself not caring. I called it: *Glory Doesn't Care*.

The Zone System

Everyone in school on those last days posed. Before then, I'd catch them at their desks working, or in the computer lab researching, or in the library reading. They never looked up. On Monday, three days of school left, they made funny faces. On Tuesday, they hugged a lot. The last day of school for seniors, the Wednesday before graduation, everyone looked right into my camera and smiled or grabbed friends and acted as if they would never see each other again—as if they were never going to have a class reunion, as if we were all going to die on graduation day. You could see the fear in their faces, masked by joy, but it was there. I snapped picture after picture even though I didn't plan on sharing any of them.

"Us! Us!" a group of jazz band girls said. *Snap*.

"Can you take a picture of us, too?" nearby vo-tech guys said. *Snap*.

"Hey, Glory! Take a picture of us, willya?" Football cheer-leaders draped all over each other. *Snap.*

On the way to lunch for the very last time, there were three girls who never liked me because of the FEMINISM IS THE RADICAL NOTION THAT WOMEN ARE PEOPLE bumper sticker on my [dad's] car, one of whom claimed this made me a dyke back in eleventh grade. "Last day at lunch! Come on. Take a shot of us buying our last crappy high school food."

I did.

But they didn't know that I focused on the chicken nug-gets, soggy fries and lump of macaroni salad on their plates instead of their clueless faces.

It would seem from this that I was popular, and with my camera, I was. My camera kept me safe. Kept me in good standing with people who wanted a picture of them-selves. Kept me behind the camera rather than in front of it. I even skipped the one group picture I should have been in for yearbook—which was the yearbook club picture. I didn't get regular senior pictures taken either. Instead, I submitted a self-portrait with my eyes closed. I had to fight to get them to include it. Luckily, the only pull I had in school was with the yearbook advisor.

The picture looked like me, dead.

I was interested in death the way Ellie was interested in sex. The less adults talked to us about things, the more we wanted to know, I guess.

Anyway, I knew that one day the picture would be accu-rate, because everyone dies.

I got my first camera from my mother for my fourth birthday. I wasn't allowed to use it, but it was mine…for the future, which, looking back, is a bizarre idea when one's mother doesn't make it to one's fifth birthday. But anyway. It was a very simple Leica M5 in a leather case. Not a digital camera. Darla O'Brien believed in film. She believed in emulsion and silver halide. She believed in something called the Zone System, which was developed by two photographers named Ansel Adams and Fred Archer around 1940.

The Zone System divided the tones in a black-and-white photograph into eleven zones between maximum black and maximum white. The challenge was to make an image that represented all eleven zones. Maximum white was 10. Maximum black was 0. Max white was blown out. Max black was nothingness.

Max black was my code for dead. "Max Black" would be what I secretly called the petrified bat because I was picky about saying something was what it wasn't. The bat was not petrified. Minerals couldn't have replaced its cells. It was just dead. Zone 0. Max black.

My one regret was that I never photographed the bat before we drank it. It would have made such a great image— so many zones represented, standing at attention, carving themselves into the emulsion. It would have represented me. Glory O'Brien, light as a feather. Glory O'Brien, jarred. Glory O'Brien, faking everyone out looking alive when really I was disintegrating. Glory O'Brien, wings folded, not flying.

I'd taken a picture of the jar, of the picnic table, of Ellie staring into the bat's mummified eyes, but I never took a shot of the bat itself. Maybe this meant something. Maybe it didn't. You choose.

Maybe I was avoiding death at the same time as I was obsessed with it.

Humans are weird, right? We're walking contradictions. We are zone 10 and zone 0 at the same time. We aren't really sure.

Or, at least, I wasn't. But that was a secret.

I loved the challenge of the Zone System, but I had never tried it. Darla's darkroom was off-limits. It was an acrid-smelling shrine in the basement where her secrets lived. And the more my own secrets emerged, the more I wanted to get into that darkroom and compare our notes.

Did she get those dizzying panic attacks too? Was this a sign?

What about not wanting to make friends?

What about not trusting people, in general? Was that normal?

What about feeling lost in the world? Lost in my own future?

What about my curiosity about what she did to herself? Why did she do it? Why did she seal the kitchen door with wet towels to spare me the gas?

Did she really spare me? Was this what *spared* felt like?

Boobs

Max Black would bring me closer to God than anyone ever did. Eventually.

Up until then, no one had ever convinced me that there was a real God. Not the priest who buried my mother when I was four years old, not my aunt Amy, who tried to school me in Catholicism after Darla died.

Because no god would make my mother put her head in the oven.

Not with me in the house.

Not on Letter *N* Day.

No god would let my dad suffer so much that he ended up resembling a hairy hot-air balloon. No god would make him ride one of those Jazzy carts at the supermarket like old people do because his knees hurt too much to walk.

He was only forty-three years old.

I was seventeen when I drank the bat with Ellie. Seventeen is the average age of one's first sexual encounter in America. I'm not sure what the average age of bat ingestion is.

The average age of childbearing in America is about twenty-five, which is when Dad and Darla had me. But nothing else about Darla and Dad was average.

Darla was a nearly famous photographer. Dad, before his present incarnation as the man on the Jazzy in the freezer aisle, was a painter. They built this house with the money Darla inherited from her mother after she died from non-microwave-oven cancer in 1990. Darla inherited $860,000, which was a lot of money. Her sister, Amy, inherited the same amount and blew it all on frivolous things. A tanning bed. Trips to Mexico. Bigger boobs. Shoes. A lot of shoes.

As sisters go, they were as opposite as Helen of Troy and Clytemnestra. Sadly, the immortal one in this case was too distracted by sales at Macy's to start the Trojan War or launch a thousand ships.

After Darla died, Aunt Amy tried for years to con me into having a First Communion in a pretty white dress. She would try to teach me about confession and sin and the Virgin Mary, but all I could see when she told me about Catholicism were her weird, round, wobbly silicone boobs.

She always wore low-cut tops.

Even when she dressed to sell God to little motherless girls.

Amy didn't come around anymore. I didn't expect a graduation card or any sort of present from her, though she did still send birthday cards—usually with overly girly motifs that made me want to puke. Amy always had a way of going over the top because I told her I was a feminist when I was twelve, and she told Dad he'd brainwashed me into being some sort of half-boy.

Which was bullshit. I was not a half-boy. I was still totally myself. I just wanted Aunt Amy to get paid as much as a man if ever she got off her lazy ass and got a job.

Why did everyone mix up that word so much?

My dad didn't brainwash me; I was simply *aware*. And from the looks of things around my high school, I was in the minority.

Ellie told me once that the feminist years were over.

"What the hell does that mean?" I'd asked.

"It means that's so 1970s or something. Twentieth-century."

I looked her up and down. "And hippie communes are twenty-first-century? Seriously?"

"You know what I mean," she said. "It's over. We got what we needed. We don't have to fight anymore."

I remember exactly what I said that day when she said that. I said, "Homeschooling is making you stupid."

But it wasn't homeschooling.

She'd said what most people really think.

Empty plastic

I hadn't always been the yearbook photographer. Halfway through senior year, they asked me to step in. Ms. Ingraham, the yearbook advisor, said she figured I'd have a good eye. She did not mention why she figured this. She did not mention that I might have inherited my eye from Darla-whose-eyes-no-longer-saw.

"John Risla was expelled," Ms. Ingraham said.

"I heard." He was a serial plagiarizer. We all knew it was coming.

"Do you think you'd like to be our yearbook photographer for the rest of the year?"

"Sure," I said. "But I don't want to be part of the club."

"But—I ..." she stammered.

"I just want to take pictures," I said. "That's all. No club."

"Okay," she said. "That would be great."

Dad supplied the camera—a digital. To make myself feel better about using a digital, I tried to shoot every yearbook picture using the Zone System.

It was totally possible. Just because it was invented by two guys who used to make their own emulsion and paint it on 20 × 24-inch glass plates in the 1940s didn't mean the Zone System couldn't be used by anyone using any kind of camera.

It was all about exposure.

While everyone else my age had their digital cameras set to automatic, I dug out Darla's old handheld light meter.

A light meter could tell you what zone everything in a scene fell into. Bright spots—waterfall foam, reflections, a polar bear—were high numbers. Shadows—holes, dark still water, eels beneath the surface—were low numbers. You had to let the light into the camera in just the right way. You had to meter: find the dark and light spots in your subject. You had to bracket: manually change your shutter speed or aperture to adjust the amount of light hitting the film—or in my case, for the yearbook, the microchip. You didn't want to blow out the highlights, and you had to give the shadows all the detail you could by finding the darkest max black areas and then shooting them three zones lighter.

By shooting the darkest areas three zones lighter, you turned a black, lifeless max black zone 0 into a zone 3.

I think, in life, most of us did this all the time.

You essentially called the woman in the oven "unhappy." You called her "frustrated." And you called the family who was left over "grieving." You called them "hanging in there." You called them "dealing with it pretty well."

Everything is about detail in the Zone System, so if you shoot a zone 0 as a zone 0, there is nothing you can do with your exposure that will bring any detail to that zone. It is max black. There is no emulsion left on the negative. All you have is empty plastic.

That's how I felt about Darla. Like empty plastic.

Dad would say, "Come on, Cupcake, it's not that bad."

I wondered if that was what he'd said to Mom on Letter *N* Day. I wondered if his meter was off. If he was accidentally reading threes where there were zeroes. Or purposefully. You choose.

Dad was a recluse outside of his trips to the grocery store, which usually happened between 2 AM and 4 AM on a random weekday night. He never seemed to think about art anymore.

Now he just made calls all day from the couch and worked on his laptop. He got paid to help people through their computer issues. I always hoped that deep in his brain he was brewing a series of German expressionist paintings of domestic gas ovens and one day he would paint it.

———

After school on Wednesday—the last day of school before graduation—I went over to see Ellie with my camera to show her the pictures I'd taken of the kids posing at me all day as if they were movie stars.

As I walked across the road, I noticed no one was really around at the commune, which was strange because a lot of people lived there. Three families in the barn, two in the old hunting cabin out back, two in the ugly blue-sided prefab, and then the RVs, three or four of them, with a family apiece.

Of course, Jasmine lived in the best house—the old farmhouse—with Ellie and Ed Heffner, Ellie's father, who I rarely saw on account of his being a hermit.

Ellie said he was shy. When I met him the few times I did, though, he just seemed annoyed. I wasn't sure what he had to be annoyed about. Dad said none of them worked. They lived off the land and got by without having to have jobs, which sounded like heaven to me. Dad said they were nonconsumerists and when I asked him what that meant he said they didn't want to buy anything.

When I found Ellie, I could tell something was wrong with her, but when I asked, she said, "I'm fine."

I didn't push because I didn't really feel like caring. She was wearing a hippie shirt with the buttons undone just to the edge of the warning zone. Like Jasmine did. It could have been Jasmine's shirt for all I knew. Jasmine could have been the one who suggested to unbutton it to that point . . . while at the same time saying *If you have sex too early, you'll regret it.*

Ellie wasn't graduating with me, so I couldn't officially celebrate my last day of school *ever* with her, but I showed her the pictures on my camera.

"Who's that?" she asked, pointing at the tall guy from jazz band.

"Travis something. Johnson. Travis Johnson," I said.

"Shit. He grew."

"And that's Morgan," I said, pointing to an old busmate of ours.

"Damn! She's punk rock. Who knew?"

"I know, right?" Morgan used to be a geek. Then she found Joey Ramone.

"Is that Danny?" Ellie asked. Danny was her secret eighth-grade crush. In the picture, his girlfriend was hugging him and kissing his cheek.

"Yep."

"Huh. He isn't as cute anymore somehow."

"Yeah. A lot changed since eighth grade," I said.

"So today was your last day?" she asked.

"Yeah."

"Why aren't you out eating at McDonald's or at the diner or something to celebrate? Like—the normal things seniors do?"

My yearbook club had invited me to the diner. But I wanted to come home on the bus one last time. (I took a picture of the interior of the bus after everyone but me and a kid named Jeff got off. I called it: *Empty Bus.*)

"Nah. I'm just glad it's over," I said.

"Why? You've been ignoring all those college letters, right? Why be happy something is over when there's nothing to go to next?"

I looked at her and frowned. "I don't know."

"Oh."

"I'll figure it out."

"You will."

I clicked forward on my camera setting and showed her *Empty Bus*.

"What's that?" she asked.

"It's the empty bus. It's, like, the last empty thing that has to do with school or something. Or it's some sort of proof that I don't have to do that anymore. I don't know. But today was the day I had to take it."

"My mom says I'll graduate over the summer sometime, maybe," she said. "They send me a real diploma and everything."

I said, "That's nice." But I was pretty sure she was lying.

Obligate parasites can't live without a host

The next morning, my first day of no-school-ever-again, I went to Ellie's. As I crossed the road I felt weird about it—I asked, *Why am I always going to Ellie's?* The answer was a shrug. *I don't know why you're going to Ellie's. You always go to Ellie's. You don't have anywhere else to go.*

I found her on her back porch, sulking.

"Last night my mom said it might take until December for me to graduate," she said. "She says I shouldn't rush the most important thing in life."

"Is that why you've been so pissed off?" I asked.

"Yeah," she answered. "And other stuff."

"Boyfriend stuff?"

"Maybe."

Ellie's boyfriend's name was Rick. He was nineteen and he'd lived on the commune since he was seven and we used to call him Ricky. He bragged that he'd had sex a lot, but Ellie and I couldn't figure out where or how because the commune was small and it wasn't like there were a ton of girls to have sex with.

"He's acting weird," she said. "Like he doesn't like me anymore." She waited a second to see if I'd say anything and when I didn't, she added, "And some of the kids have lice and I can't stand lice."

"Bummer," I said, because lice on the commune was more common than lavender bushes, knitting, or basmati rice. I backed away. I think this is a normal human reaction.

She scowled. "It's not like I have them! Geez!"

"It's lice. They jump. I learned it in health class."

"Lice don't jump."

"Oh," I said, still keeping my head at least a meter from her head.

"Fleas jump. Lice crawl."

She said it like it was a normal thing to be talking about. *Fleas jump. Lice crawl.* I said, "You can't blame me for not wanting to get lice. Who wants lice?"

"I don't have them! I just know we all have to be careful because some of the kids have them." She started to cry a little. "I'm so fucking sick of this shit, you know that?"

I thought she meant me, so I kept my mouth shut. Ever since Rick showed up in her life, I was hoping she'd get sick of me. I'd even daydreamed about starting a new life somewhere else, anywhere else. A place where no one knew about Darla and no one would seem insensitive for not talking to me about it.

"The minute I turn eighteen, I'm getting the hell out of here. With Rick, maybe. He's getting out, too. And we can get our GEDs and won't have to homeschool anymore."

I nodded but didn't offer a hug. Lice spread somehow. It's a fact.

"Are you itchy?" I asked, pointing to my head.

"I've had so much tea tree oil in my hair since Mom told me, I'm hoping they just stay away."

Ellie gave me lice twice as a kid—the last time when we were eleven years old. Dad and I washed and dried every linen in the house on high heat and then put them in the microwave oven for five minutes to make sure.

Microwave ovens are like atomic bombs to lice.

"Are you coming to my graduation Monday?" I asked.

I'd asked this twelve times before. I'd given her the invitation the day I got them. I got four. I still had two left over, and was thinking of putting one in the mail with no return address. *Darla O'Brien, Heaven or Hell, You Choose, The Universe, 00000.*

"My mom hasn't made up her mind. She says I can go, but she can't figure out how I'll get there. The van will be out for a day trip."

"I can drive you if you don't mind hanging around for a while," I said.

"I think she's planning a star party for the same night, so I may not be able to get out of that," Ellie said. She tried to look sad about it, but star parties were the one thing she loved about the commune. They had them every other week in summer—or whenever the planets did something exciting. Ellie could tell you every constellation in the sky. It got annoying.

"So what are you gonna do about those if you have them?" I asked, pointing to her head.

She scratched her head. "I'll probably ask you to get some of that drugstore stuff for me. Would that be okay?"

"Sure," I said. "Because those little fuckers are using us, you know."

"Yeah."

"Obligate parasites can't live without a host."

"Okay, Professor."

"Did you know they came from gorillas, like, two million years ago?"

"Really?"

"Actually, I think that was pubic lice."

"Ew," she said.

"Yep."

"Does that mean some human had sex with a gorilla?"

"I think it was just lice to gorillas. It only became pubic lice to us because we lost our body fur. Uh. Well. Most of it, anyway."

We sat down on the grass and then lay back to look at the sky. It was clear with a few high clouds. Since I could remember, we would play the cloud game; we'd say they looked like animals or other shapes and then we'd watch them morph into other animals or things until they drifted out of view and were replaced by new ones.

"Are you gonna shave yours off?" she asked.

"What?"

"You know—your hair," she said. "Down there."

"Uh—no."

She sighed.

"Why?" I asked.

"A lot of people do, I guess."

"Does Rick want you to?" I asked.

She didn't answer.

"I don't know," I said. "Just seems unnatural."

She didn't answer and we lay there looking at the clouds some more.

"Have you seen Jupiter this week?" she asked. When I shook my head no, she said, "You should. Just go outside at about ten and look southeast. Can't miss it. It's blue and really bright."

"Okay," I said. But I didn't care about Jupiter.

"Markus is coming home from college today," she said. Markus Glenn, porn perv, lived down the road from us. He used to take the yellow school bus until he transferred to a private school in sixth grade. "You still crush on him, don't you?"

"Not since seventh grade, no," I said. "Remember?"

She nodded. "Did you know nearly every serial killer in history had a porn addiction? Helped them dehumanize people so they could kill them," she said.

"You didn't learn that at homeschool."

"Rick told me. He's got all these books about serial killers."

"Wow. That's not creepy at all."

"Stop it."

"Okay," I said, but I still thought it was creepy.

Say that in a sheep voice

Star parties were a big deal on the commune. They'd bring out their drums and play beats for the stars. They'd eat organic treats and drink elderberry cordial. They would dress up.

It was all very special.

Jupiter had been around for a few months and visible every night. But cool things were happening with the moon and Pluto or something, so Jasmine called the party and the commune answered a bleating "Yes, please."

Say that in a sheep voice.

My dad did.

It's not that he didn't like the commune people. He just thought they were flaky and he didn't like that they would drum through the night during solstice or equinox or star parties.

There was something deeper going on, but I hadn't figured it out. I had this feeling that Jasmine Blue hadn't been very sympathetic after Letter *N* Day.

She'd never mentioned Darla once—nor my father, which was weird because he was still alive. In my seventeen years, thirteen without Mom, my dad and Jasmine Blue had never talked on the phone or seen each other even though they lived across the road.

Dad would pretend he didn't know who I meant unless I said "Ellie's mom."

He would use the term himself, too.

"Does Ellie's mom think it's okay for you two to be walking on the road to Markus's house at your age?" (We were twelve.)

"Does Ellie's mom have a landline in case I need to get ahold of you?"

Jasmine made me keep my cell phone at home. Cell phones caused cancer. We were all talking into atomic bombs.

We all had our collective heads in the oven.

———

As Ellie and I cloudbusted for an hour, I watched cloud after cloud go by and saw each one as an oven. Sometimes the door was open. Sometimes the door was closed. Sometimes there was a pie baking inside. I thought of the pie as my future. I thought of the pie as an impossible goal. I knew from experience that microwaved pies tasted like shit.

When Ellie asked me a second time about college, I told her I just wanted some space. This was a lie. The real reason was tucked deep inside my brain and Ellie wasn't going to find out. Especially considering that sometimes, it was hard to tell where Ellie stopped and where Jasmine began.

I went home and ate dinner. Chicken Alfredo and soggy garlic bread. Dad said he had to work, so I ate alone in the kitchen. Last day of school. Ever.

Being alone at the dinner table made me feel like I was in zone *whatever*. I had no idea who I was or what to think. I took a picture of the chair that Dad usually sat in. Its upholstery was falling apart and I'd asked Dad to replace it ten times by now, but he wouldn't. I named the picture *Ugly, Empty Chair*.

———

When I was done, I wandered back to Ellie's house. They'd already eaten dinner and Jasmine told me that Ellie was out with her chickens doing her chores. As I walked toward the chicken house, I passed by the shed where the bat was. I wondered if it had disintegrated yet, in that confining jar we put it in. I wondered, if it was really God, then why were we ignoring it? I decided to ask Ellie about it when I found her.

But then, as I neared the chicken house, I heard voices. It was Rick and Ellie.

As I got closer, I heard them yelling at each other.

"But it sucks! You don't get it!"

"I'm not getting pregnant, Rick."

"Other girls let me do it all the time."

"Other girls?"

"I mean *before* you."

"Even more of a reason for you to wear one," Ellie said.

"You just don't get it."

"I guess I don't. But I know I'm not getting pregnant at seventeen. That, I know." Her voice wobbled on "that." Like maybe she was going to cry.

"I can pull out right before."

That's when I decided to walk in.

Ellie stood, leaning against a pitchfork. Rick had a bale of straw at his feet.

I said, "Hi there."

Rick looked mad.

Ellie looked like she didn't know what a woman was supposed to look like.

When neither of them answered me, I decided I really didn't want to be there for this. Ellie would talk about it for hours later when we were alone, so I turned around and went home.

I figured maybe I had something better to do than just hang around at Ellie's like a bad habit.

Dad was still sitting on the couch working on his laptop. I stared at the painting above his head—a huge canvas he'd painted—of a modest nude.

Woman. That's what he titled the painting.

Throughout my life, whenever a TV commercial came on that involved a skimpily clad girl, he'd point to the painting and say, "Glory, don't believe what you see." He'd point. "That's what a real woman looks like." Or something like that.

I couldn't remember how long he'd been saying this to me, but I couldn't remember a time when he wasn't saying it, so I bet it was since the very beginning. It was all he'd ever say when I'd turn on the TV. Wrinkle cream. Makeup. Clothing. Nail polish. Posh chocolates. Cars. Beer. Sofas. Shampoo. Toothpaste. Casinos. Gym memberships. Shoes. Pills. Diets. Cat food. Every commercial that tried to sell me the real world that wasn't real, he'd point and say it.

The woman in the painting was fleshy and had hips. She was thick legged. Her breasts had real shape—not like Aunt Amy's squishy softballs. She didn't have ridiculously long eyelashes and she didn't have tan lines. She just *was*.

"You need me?" Dad said.

"Just looking at the woman," I said. I'd wondered for years if the woman in the painting was Darla, but I knew Darla didn't look like her at all. Darla was skinny and had long hair she often tied into braided pigtails.

"You okay?" he asked.

"Never better," I lied.

"You doing anything fun tomorrow?" he asked.

"Sure. Fun," I said, and went upstairs and made a pact with myself not to go to Ellie's the next day. I remembered the line about habits. The first step to breaking one is admitting you have a problem.

I had other things to do. I'd taken so many pictures in the last week, I wanted to get them into my sketchbook.

I had three sketchbooks now—full of computer-printed digital pictures. I wished I could print real pictures but Dad still wouldn't let me into Darla's darkroom and the last time I'd asked, he looked so hurt I couldn't bring myself to push it.

I'd named this sketchbook *The Origin of Everything*. Dad had given me a blank sketchbook every year for Christmas and my birthday since I started taking pictures. He showed me one he made back when he still cared about art. It was a mix of everything creative—pictures, drawings, ideas, writing. He said it would help me work out my feelings. I didn't ask him why he didn't keep sketchbooks anymore. It was obvious he wasn't working out anything.

The Origin of Everything was almost finished. I only had a few more pages to fill.

I printed and pasted *Empty Jar*. Beneath it I wrote *EMPTY JAR*.

I printed and pasted *Empty Bus*. Beneath it I wrote *NO SEAT BELTS*.

I printed and pasted *Ugly, Empty Chair*. Beneath it I wrote *NEEDS NEW UPHOLSTERY*.

I printed and pasted a random picture of a group of seniors who'd asked me to take their picture the day before. I wrote *THIS IS WHAT NORMAL PEOPLE LOOK LIKE*.

When I slipped into bed, I thought about how even though *Woman* wasn't Darla, she was somehow teaching me stuff all along. I still thought about the fight I'd heard between Ellie and Rick. I didn't think about college or getting a job. I didn't think about anything past tomorrow because anything past tomorrow was just like cloudbusting—it depended solely upon the person looking at the clouds and it could rain any minute.

Saturday–It's complicated

I'd been up since dawn taking pictures of tiny things with my macro lens. I captured dewdrops. I captured pollen. Insects. Moss. I took a picture of a dead beetle. I called it *Dead Beetle*. I took a picture of my pinkie toe. I called it *Dad Says I Have My Mother's Feet*.

When I looked at small things—macro things—the big picture faded away.

I sat down in the hammock and balanced and then lay back. When I did, I realized that when one is looking up through trees at the sky, there is nothing a macro lens can capture. Nothing small. I took a picture of the view with my lens turned back to standard. I called it *Nothing Small*.

It was two days before my graduation from high school and I was more worried about Ellie than I was about getting a dress. I wanted to talk to her about the argument I'd overheard in the chicken house two nights before. I worried about how girls buckle.

Jasmine Blue didn't allow a television in her house, so Ellie had never been desensitized to the commercials and stereotypes. Jasmine Blue didn't allow magazines in her house, but Ellie knew what all girls knew—we were here to be whatever men wanted us to be.

We were here to touch their tipis.

I tried to think of one single message out there that said the opposite, but I couldn't think of one. Everywhere I'd looked for seventeen years said, under the slick imagery, "You are here to look pretty, keep quiet, and touch tipis."

I didn't want Ellie to get pregnant. I wanted her to be educated about sex and how much bullshit "pulling out" was. I didn't want her to catch a sexually transmitted disease from a guy who owned books about serial killers.

I waited in the hammock until eight thirty to go and find Ellie. I found her mucking out the runner duck house that was over by the small pond. She still looked mad, so it was a perfect opportunity to just ask her if she was okay.

"I'm fine. Why?"

"You look pissed."

"I *am* pissed. But I'm fine," she said. "Just the usual bullshit."

"What usual bullshit?"

She propped her chin on the handle of her shovel and sighed. The ducks ran around outside. Runner ducks walk upright. She had two different colors of them. The chocolate-colored ones were my favorite.

"Just—you know—Rick. It's complicated."

I nodded. "I heard a little bit of your fight Thursday," I said. "I didn't like what he was saying to you."

She sighed again.

"You know about safe sex, right? And diseases? And all that?"

"I know enough," she said.

"Well—uh—be careful, will you?" I wished I could take her to the library and hand her over to the librarians. *Please teach her about everything*, I'd say.

A minute passed and I picked up the broom and swept out some wood shavings from the corner.

"I think my mom was right," she said. "I did it too early and now I regret it."

I felt my heart stop for a second. "You *did* it?"

We'd promised, on that day when we found the picture of the butter penis, that we would tell each other on the day we did it. I felt cheated, like I did every other time Ellie changed the rules.

She nodded. "Like, two weeks ago. I mean, the first time. We've been doing it since, too. I'm sorry I didn't tell you."

"But I thought you weren't going to do it."

"It's not a big deal," she said.

"Then why are you so mad?" I let that echo around the duck house for a few seconds. I said, "You can stop anytime you want."

"He lives here."

"So?"

"It's complicated."

"Yeah. I can see that. But still."

She started to cry. "I don't know what to do."

I didn't know what to tell her.

I hugged her even though lice spread somehow.

I didn't care. Ellie needed a hug so I hugged her.

"And I have bad news," she said.

"Oh?" I said.

"My mom found the petrified bat."

"Did she toss it?"

"Not quite. I still have it. But it's...not like we remember it."

The ballad of Max Black (aka God)

It was dust. No matter how closely we looked, we couldn't distinguish what used to be eyeball or wing or snout or foot. It was just chunky dust.

Ellie acted out what Jasmine had done.

"*'What the hell is this?'*" she said in an annoying-Jasmine voice, while shaking the jar, disintegrating Max Black. "She just kept shaking it and yelling," she said. "She's such a freak. It's just a bat. Like, who cares?"

"It wasn't just a bat," I said.

"I know," Ellie said. "It was God."

"Your mom killed God, dude," I said. I was trying to get a laugh, but Ellie didn't laugh.

She unscrewed the lid to the jar and she looked in at the dust.

I think that's when she got the idea, but she didn't say anything until we met later—after dark—to give our God, Max Black, a proper journey into the next bat world by scattering his dust.

Once we met, skinny waxing moon high in the sky, that's not what we did at all.

Ellie said, "I need you to get that lice stuff for me."

"Okay." My scalp itched the minute she said it. "Bummer. I know how much you hate those combs." Last time Ellie had lice, she had to chop a foot off her hair so she could get the nit comb through it.

"They moved," she said.

"Who?"

"The lice."

"But," I said. "Head lice only live on heads."

"They—you know—*moved*." She pointed to the zipper on her jeans.

"El, that's an entirely different thing. They didn't spread. Those are different ones."

"You thought they jumped until last week. What do you know?"

"I know."

"Oh."

"So, your head is okay?"

"Yeah. It's fine," she said. "Hold on. So I have a different kind now?" she asked.

"Sounds like it."

"Where the fuck did they come from?"

I stayed quiet.

"Rick?"

"That's how they spread, I guess," I said.

"Then where'd *he* get them?"

I didn't say anything.

"We've been dating for three months."

I didn't say anything.

"Is this the shit we caught off gorillas?"

"I think there are a lot of different species. But yeah. Pretty much, I think," I said. "Do you want me to get enough stuff for both of you?"

"No fucking thank you."

"Does this mean it's over with Rick?"

"Yes fucking please."

That was going to be complicated.

But we soon forgot about it when she went into the shed and produced the jar, the dust of the god Max Black, and a six-pack of beer.

The clan of the petrified bat

Ellie was in zone 1 all night. She said "Who gives a fuck?" a lot.

I asked, "So, where are we going?"

Ellie said, "Who gives a fuck?"

We headed to the pond because I didn't want to drink beer in my woods. When we got there and I unfurled a blanket I'd brought from home, I asked Ellie, "You want to sit on the blanket or just the grass?"

Ellie said, "Who gives a fuck?"

I laid the blanket out and sat down on it. I pulled out a small bag of Doritos and offered her one and she glared at me.

"What?" I asked.

"You're always so fucking prepared." She sat down on the blanket and added, "You and your fluorescent orange food." I didn't have time to say anything before she looked on the verge of tears and said, "What the hell can a six-pack of beer do for my problems? You know?" She pointed to the zipper of her jeans again.

"I don't know. Where'd you get it, anyway?"

"Rick, remember?"

"I mean the six-pack."

"I got that from Rick too. We were going to drink it during the star party on Monday. But now, who gives a fuck?"

"I'll get you stuff tomorrow and they'll be gone and you won't have to worry about it anymore. It won't be your problem."

"It will always be my problem," she said. "My *problem* is that I'm an idiot. My *problem* is that we're all idiots. You and me and my mom and everyone I live with and everyone we know and everyone who lives on this road, in this town and in the state and the country and everyone on the planet. That's my fucking problem."

"Shit," I said.

"Yeah. Shit," she said.

Ellie kept a scowl on her face as we drank our first beers. I stayed quiet and let her hold court. She talked more about how the world was full of idiots, mostly.

When we cracked open our second beers, I said, "Do you mind if I say something?"

"No."

"I think something's wrong with me," I said.

"Like what?" She said it in a way that made it clear that right at that moment, even if I had leprosy or cancer, nothing was going to be worse than her case of regretful sex and crab lice, so I clammed up.

"Nothing," I said. "I'm just being weird."

Silence took over.

We drank some more beer, though neither of us seemed to like it all that much. I put mine down and didn't plan on picking it up again. Then Ellie fidgeted a bit and muttered some stuff under her breath. She turned to me and said, "Someone else had to give them to him, right?"

"Yeah. Pretty much."

"I am such a dipshit," she said.

"You're not a dipshit," I said.

As we lay and looked at the stars, Ellie stirred herself into more and more crab-anger. I thought maybe she was going to get up and leave me there. I thought she was about to combust. She wasn't herself—none of the facets of Ellie I knew. Not the silly or the sarcastic or the oddly Jasmine-like. She was just... so pissed off. I'd seen her pissed off before, sure, but not like this. This was deeper.

"I think we should drink the fucking thing," she said.

I'd zoned out and had no idea what she was talking about, so I said, "What?"

"The petrified bat. God. Whatever you want to call that shit," she said, pointing to the jar.

"Max Black," I said.

"Max Black?"

"That's what I call it. It's a photography term. Ignore me. I think I'm getting drunk."

Ellie held up the jar. "I'll go first," she said. "We'll grow wings. It'll be like drinking God. Hell. Maybe it'll even give us a buzz." She leaned over and took the last half beer—technically my beer, but it was warm and I didn't want to drink it.

She opened the jar and smelled the contents first. "It's just dust. It won't even taste like anything." Then she poured the beer over the dust and swirled the mix around until it homogenized the best it could.

She drank first—made a face like it was delicious, and then handed it to me.

I hesitated and then I drank, confidently. What did I have to lose, right? I was about to graduate from high school and had nowhere to go and nothing better to do. Why not drink the remains of a bat? Some of it spilled down the side of my neck because the jar's mouth was so big. I swallowed it and washed it back with the last of the warm beer in my bottle.

Ellie held out her arms, palms up. "It's like we're part of God now, isn't it, Glory?"

I'd only mentioned the God stuff before as a joke, but Ellie seemed to really *feel* it or something. I felt pretty light-headed. I figured I was a little tipsy and had too much drink-the-bat adrenaline running around my system. But sure—this feeling could pass for being God. Glory O'Brien. God. Owned an atomic bomb. Daughter of long-dead Darla O'Brien, max black.

I looked at Ellie. Ellie Heffner. God. Did not own an atomic bomb, unless you count the pubic lice treatment I was about to buy for her. Daughter of Jasmine Blue Heffner, hippie weirdo freak.

"We're a clan now. It's like being blood sisters, but better. Clan of the petrified bat!" Ellie slurred.

Then everything changed, only we didn't know it yet.

———

I felt like I wanted to puke for about a half hour after we drank it. I'd only ever had one other beer before, so I didn't know what it was like to be drunk. I'd never felt quite like *that*, though.

Ellie looked like she really believed she was God. She whispered to herself a little, like she was having a conversation with someone. Maybe the crabs. Maybe herself. Maybe she was just drunk. On God.

"Free yourself," Ellie said. "Have the courage."

"What?"

"Free yourself. Have the courage," she repeated. "I don't know. It just came to me."

I answered, "Oh." I didn't know if she was saying it to me or to herself.

I thought about that. *Free yourself. Have the courage.* It had so many meanings. So many accusations for me.

We lay looking up at the stars for what seemed like an hour and Ellie didn't tell me one constellation for once. She didn't even point out Jupiter. It bothered me so much I nearly pointed it out myself.

But then I looked at it, and I saw its history and its future all at once.

I saw a huge explosion. I saw the planets and stars each

take their place in the blackness. I saw the speed of light. Then darkness again—as if everything had died. It made me want to cry.

So I looked away.

I looked at Ellie and she looked frightened.

Maybe she saw what I saw.

"I should go," I said. Just like that. I was lying there, then I was standing, waiting for her to get off my blanket. When she got up, Ellie said a hushed good-bye.

I walked home and said hi to Dad. I didn't look at him, though. I felt like if I did, he'd see I was some sick girl who'd just drunk the remains of a mummified bat. Maybe he'd see I was God.

It was confusing.

I went to bed with all my clothes on, trying to focus on feeling normal. I did not feel normal. I felt like I was floating. Flying. Lighter and heavier at the same time.

Twoooeee-toooo-tooo-tooo

I woke up at five to the sound of the mourning dove that lives near my bedroom window. I never liked mourning doves. I knew what mourning was, and the bird wasn't mourning.

The window was about six feet high by ten feet wide and was separated into three sections. Just outside my window there was a line of flowering fruit trees. The mourning dove sat in one of them, singing that horrible song. *Twoooeee-toooo-tooo-tooo.*

When I looked at the bird, I saw things.

Strange things.

I saw its ancestors. I saw its great-great-great-grandfather getting hit by a car, feathers exploding in all directions. I saw its children. I saw its great-grandchildren. I saw the bird's infinity all the way to extinction. To dust.

Just like I'd seen Jupiter the night before.

I felt that familiar panic. I shook my head and stretched my shoulders back to relieve the tightness in my chest.

Today was going to be normal and I was going to buy a dress for graduation at the mall. Very simple. Maybe later, I'd meet up with Ellie and say something like "Whoa, that was weird, eh?" and we'd laugh.

Ah ha ha ha ha.

I took a shower. I did the thing my dad taught me when I was little when my brain would move too fast. I kept the bathroom light off. I tried not to think of anything except the water hitting my face. I tried to *be there*. I breathed in and out. I smiled. I did neck rolls. I felt the water hitting my face. I smiled again.

I still felt wrong. I felt like Max Black the bat. I felt invisible wings in my back. I felt like eating bugs. I could hear for miles.

I was different.

More neck rolls. Water hitting my face. Smile. *Glory, don't be so dramatic.*

———

I stuck my camera (the Leica M5 with black-and-white film) in my bag in case I wanted to stop and shoot pictures on my way to the mall to buy a dress. Sometimes I did that. I considered it a family heirloom—claiming time alone exploring shit that no one else found interesting. Carving those interesting things into real negatives. I considered it my right.

Darla O'Brien stuck her head in an oven, so now I got to

pretend I was her sometimes. Whatever she was. Whoever she was. I got to pretend like I knew. *Twoooeee-toooo-tooo-tooo.*

Dad was settling into the couch when I left. He talked to me as I washed out my cereal bowl in the kitchen.

"You okay?"

"Yeah. Going for the dumb dress," I said.

"You don't *have* to wear a dress, you know," he said. I could see Darla saying that. Or maybe she wouldn't.

"I know."

"Good."

Truth is, I didn't know what else girls wore to be dressy. I didn't want to wear some business suit or anything. I figured I could just go to the mall and look and then if I couldn't find anything, I could stop at the vintage thrift store on the way home and buy one of those 1940s housedresses. Something casual and roomy. Something I could wear with Doc Martens shoes and no one would care.

Everyone already thought I was weird. *Glory O'Brien, voted Most Likely to Not Be Your Friend. Glory O'Brien, voted Most Likely Not to Touch Your Tipi. Glory O'Brien, voted Most Likely to Stick Her Head in an Oven.*

When I parked in front of Sears, a car pulled into the space beside me and I looked at the driver and she looked at me and I saw a . . . vision. A whole bunch of them, actually.

Transmission from the woman parking next to me: *Her mother was in jail. Her grandmother loved jazz. Her grandson will flunk out of high school. Her other grandson will become a senator and finally get equal pay for women in the workplace. It will be the middle of the twenty-first century. That senator will have a second home in Arizona, and the day he brings that bill to the Senate floor in Washington, DC, people in Arizona will burn his other house down.*

I looked away from the driver and shook my head.

That was insane.

Maybe you are insane.

You broke.

Like Darla.

Twoooeee-toooo-tooo-tooo.

The driver didn't even notice I'd been staring at her. I don't think I was. I think the transmission—it came in like a second or less.

I walked toward the front door of Sears convinced that I was imagining things. No way does drinking a dead bat make you hallucinate that much—to see other people's futures or pasts or whatever. I'd read about frogs you can lick and mushrooms you can eat and other crazy shit like nutmeg. No bats.

Nothing about bats.

The big joke was

It didn't get any better inside the mall. I looked down mostly, but when I dared look at a person, I could see their ancestors and descendants. I could see events in their past and their future. I could see their infinity, I guess.

Example.

Transmission from the guy arguing at the cashier desk at Sears: *His great-great-great-grandfather was a slave on a plantation in Alabama and was abused endlessly by the men he worked for. He killed two of them with his bare hands before he was beaten to death in punishment. That man's son was also a slave. His great-grandfather knew freedom, but not from anger and abuse. His grandfather moved north but still wasn't free. His father rioted in Newark in 1967. He lit houses on fire. No transmission from the future. The man has no children.*

Shit.

I knew I had to walk through Sears to get to the Dress-barn, so I looked down and walked fast. Once I escaped Sears, I walked over the bridge that spans a fountain. The fountain was made famous by a YouTube video of some woman who was so busy texting that she fell right in. If you saw that video, then you know the fountain outside Sears.

The bridge has these wooden benches next to it. I sat on one of them and went into my purse for a penny. If ever there was a day for a wish, I was in it.

I tossed it in and closed my eyes. *I wish that I'm not going crazy like Darla.*

The Dressbarn was on the left side of the mall next to the Orange Julius and a blacked-out storefront that used to be the Build-A-Bear Workshop. As I crossed over toward Dressbarn, I saw a little kid walking from potted plant to potted plant in the center of the mall. She had to touch every pot with her hand in some sort of OCD-like kid ritual.

Transmission from little girl at the mall: *Her son will become a doctor who goes to countries where disasters happen. He will go to China. He will go to Italy. He will go to Syria. He will go to Congo and Zimbabwe. He will be nominated for a peace prize, but will not win it.*

I watched the girl weave in and out of the potted plants until I couldn't see her anymore. I could feel the kids working at Orange Julius staring at me. I looked back at the floor and then walked into Dressbarn.

I found a cool seersucker cotton dress in my size. It almost looked like one of those 1940s housedresses, but it was shorter and had some shape to it. I took it off the rack in a size larger, too, and headed to the dressing room. Only when I got inside and sat on the small stool did I realize that there were two mirrors there.

Maybe if I looked at myself I'd see things I'd never want to see. Or maybe my great-granddaughter would be some awesome woman who would cure cancer or AIDS or something.

Or maybe I'd find out about Darla's parents and their parents and theirs and theirs until I got all the way back to some small damp village in Eastern Europe where her ancestors met.

Or maybe I'd find out what really happened to Darla. In her head. Maybe I would stop having to make up reasons for what she did. If there were reasons.

When I got the courage, I looked in the mirror and I saw nothing. I got no transmissions. I got no glimpse of my future or my past. I just saw me—twenty-four hours from graduating high school, not free, not courageous.

Glory O'Brien, atomic bomb

I **bought the dress**—the larger size, because I wanted it to look roomy, like those dresses in Dorothea Lange's Farm Security Administration pictures from the Dust Bowl. Wearing clothing a size big makes you look like you're hungry and poor. Makes you look like you are withering.

When I stopped at the drugstore on the way out of the mall, I stood in aisle six pretending to look at shampoo. I asked myself, *Why am I buying crab killer for Ellie? Why can't she do it herself?* And I was angry. Suddenly. One minute, I was Glory O'Brien, dress shopper; next minute I was Glory O'Brien, atomic bomb.

Somehow, staring at the nine million different types of Pantene shampoo made me see Ellie for what she'd always been. A manipulator. A competitor. A codependent. A leech. An obligate parasite—who needed me, but whom I didn't need.

Transmission from the bottle of Pantene Pro-V Straight to Curly 2-in-1: *My shampoo will make men look at you. Trust me. Wash. Rinse. Repeat.*

Transmission from the bottle of Pantene Pro-V Frizzy to Smooth shampoo: *Don't use that two-in-one shit. Makes your hair all wiry. Use me. Grab a bottle of conditioner, too, and then men will totally look at you. Also, wear shorter shorts and unbutton your blouses about two more buttons. You may also want to get a tan. And shave your legs more often.*

I took a picture of the rows of shampoo. I called it *Empty Promises.*

I walked back to the pharmacy and asked the guy for whatever would kill the pubic lice my slutty friend had. I said, "Can you give me whatever stuff will kill the pubic lice my slutty friend got?"

This made the people working in the pharmacy laugh and soon I was walking out of the mall with a graduation dress and crab killer. And I was mad at Ellie for being sexy. Or being slutty. Or being whatever made her have sex before I did. But when I looked out to the parking lot and accidentally met eyes with a guy who was walking toward me holding his son's hand, I stopped.

Transmission from the guy walking into the mall: *His grandfather was a teacher. His granddaughter will be a teacher, too, but before she ever gets a chance to teach, she will be exiled from a place called New America.* I shook my head and walked to my car.

When I got there, I stared at myself in the sun visor's

mirror until I could get a transmission. No transmission. *See, Glory? You're imagining things.*

––––––––

When I got home I took a deep breath and approached Dad.

"You're staring at me," Dad said.

"Yes," I said.

Transmission from Dad: *His great-great-grandfather came to America from Tipperary after losing his land to the English during the 1888 evictions. His name was Pádraig O'Brien and he played the tin whistle and made a living out of that and thieving in the Philadelphia area until he settled down with Mary Helen, a woman who had fourteen children, one of whom was Dad's great-grandfather John. John O'Brien was a banker ... or a thief, depending on which way you looked at it.*

He said, "Did you find the dress?"

"Oh," I said. "Yeah. I did."

"Good."

"Yeah."

He smiled at me. "You're still staring," he said.

Transmission from Dad: *His grandmother stopped talking to her sister after the farm got split up and she didn't get as much money as her sister did.*

I got no transmissions from the future. All I saw were distant cousins and grandparents and even ancestors from the fifteenth century eating a skewered, smoked pig with their dirty hands.

No future. Because maybe I had no future.

I looked down at my hands.

"Do you have something to say?" Dad asked.

"Yeah." Silence. "I know you said no before, but can I . . . can I have the key to Mom's darkroom?"

He looked surprised when I asked, as if I hadn't been taking pictures nonstop for the last few years, filling his biannual sketchbook gifts. As if I hadn't been having to take my black-and-white negatives to the local photo lab to get them sent out to be developed rather than doing it right downstairs where there was a place to do it myself.

I decided to stop all eye contact and look into space while talking to him. I didn't care about ancient O'Briens and their weird family issues.

"I want to develop some film and it seems dumb to send it out."

Dad said, "I haven't been in that darkroom since—uh." He stopped and sighed. He really thought about it as if I'd just asked him to do something huge rather than hand over a key. "I know she kept all her notebooks on the shelf above the sink. Sketchbooks . . . kind of like yours. You should find a lot of info in there. Recipes and stuff." He fidgeted, looking frazzled by this. "Chemical recipes. Not cakes. Your mother was very private about her chemistry." He gestured to the prints on the walls. "If you get into those notebooks, you can't tell anyone what's in there, okay? Especially not that Wilson dick." Mr. Wilson was the photo teacher in school. Since he got a bank of computers for his graphic arts lab, he only kept one tiny old darkroom for the history of photography class. I knew Dad hated the guy. They knew each other before. *Before.*

"No problem," I said. "I don't have any more classes with him anyway." I cleared my throat and said this last part loudly and slowly. *"Because I graduate from high school tomorrow."*

He stopped working on his laptop and looked at me.

"Wow," he said.

"Yeah."

"Jesus, how did that happen?" he asked. He took off his glasses and wiped them on his T-shirt. "Come here."

I sat next to him on the couch and he put me in a loving headlock. "How the hell are you graduating from high school already?"

"I did this thing called growing up. What happens is your body and brain get larger. It's an amazing process. You should try it."

"Smartass."

"And?"

"And I'm proud of you," he said. He let me out of the headlock.

"Is something wrong with your eye?"

He cleaned his glasses again and blinked back tears that welled in his eyes. "I worry."

I shrugged.

"No college. No plans. What the hell are you going to do here with your old man?" I didn't say anything because I didn't have an answer. "You're not sticking around for my sake, right? You better not be sticking around for my sake."

"I have a plan," I said, thinking of how I didn't really have a plan.

How could I tell Dad that I didn't make plans because I was Glory O'Brien, girl with no future? A year ago when my classmates were perusing college catalogs and course descriptions, I was just thinking about freedom. *Freedom from everything.* I didn't know what that was yet, but I knew it meant something.

I used to think it meant I was going to follow in Darla's footsteps. I knew it, you know? I knew it. But now it might mean *Free yourself. Have the courage.*

He handed me the key off his key ring. "Be careful down there."

"Bears?"

"Stop it. I'm being serious. You can't spend too much time in a darkroom, kid. It can get to you."

Why people take pictures

Zone 5. It's called middle gray. That's how I felt in Darla's darkroom.

Middle gray.

Not black, not white. Just middle gray.

Zone 5 is 50% gray. If I metered me, middle gray, in Darla's darkroom, I would be 50% Darla. Halfway toward putting my head in the oven, I guess. I mean, I'd never felt suicidal. Was that how she felt? *Not-suicidal?* Because maybe she didn't and maybe I wasn't and maybe we weren't anything alike.

Once I got into Darla's darkroom, I turned on the big light, not the darkroom amber, and hoisted myself onto the countertop where I could just sit and breathe and forget about everything I'd seen that morning. Maybe if I stayed in the darkroom forever, I'd never have to see anyone's infinity ever again.

I was finally here. It smelled like a mix of chemicals, but mostly a pungency that reminded me of the way the locker room smelled at school. Bad, but not strong. Or strong, but not bad. Pick one.

On one shelf there were huge flat boxes of photo paper that would now be over thirteen years old. Darla used all high-quality fiber paper—nothing resin coated or plastic. I knew from Dad that her recipes were attempts to double the lifetime of her images.

Ironic, isn't it?

Darla worked tirelessly to make pictures live longer and all of her pictures outlived her.

Oh well.

So, there were boxes of old paper, big jugs of old chemistry and all the darkroom equipment a girl could want. Three enlargers—one huge one that had its own stand and two regular-sized enlargers on the counter. Trays to fit up to 20 x 24-inch prints and tiny ones for 4 x 5-inch negatives. Squeegees. Tongs. Film tanks. Aquarium heaters for keeping developer warm. Plastic graduates of every size. A print washer. A print dryer that she'd made herself.

Everything. Everything was here. Darla was here.

The sketchbooks watched me from their shelf above the big steel sink.

I stared at them and wondered why I'd really care about crazy recipes for selenium toner or platinum developing or whatever. I stared at them and wondered what images she chose to paste into hers. Would they be anything like mine?

It was scary suddenly having the answers accessible to me. I just wanted to work in here. Make it my own. Make it Glory's darkroom. Wipe out the one secret place of Darla's in this house. I wanted her gone so I didn't have to wonder anymore. I wanted her here to show me how to do it. I wanted both things.

I wanted neither thing, really. I'd rather have been part of a boring family of suit-wearing certified public accountants. A mother and a father. No secret darkroom necessary.

My phone rang.

"Do you have it?" Ellie asked.

"Oh shit," I said. "Yeah. Sorry. It was a weird day."

"I know, right?" she answered. I didn't know what she meant by this, but I wondered if maybe she was seeing things, too. The future. The past. Bat-vision.

"Come over and get it, okay? I can't stop what I'm doing."

"Are you seeing it? When you look at people?" she said.

"Just come over."

I reached up to a stack of Darla's notebooks and pulled them down onto the counter. There were three of them. Two had mostly notes about chemistry. Metol, sodium hydroxide, potassium bromide, hydroquinone, sodium thiosulfate, acetic acid, boric acid, etc. I can't say I was all that interested in chemistry.

Her other sketchbook was just like Dad's and just like mine. Pictures taped in, captions written underneath. I set it aside because I wanted to read it later. Not now. Not with Ellie coming over.

I walked around the room and touched things knowing that I was touching what she would have touched. I opened the door to the print dryer. I closed it again. I opened the two cabinets under the sink and found thirteen years' worth of dust and scattered mouse droppings. I turned the knobs on the enlargers and made the bellows open and close. I saw a cabinet mounted high on the wall behind the enlargers and I stood on the stool to reach it. It was mostly more darkroom equipment. More chemistry. But then I saw the corner of something black poking out from behind the cabinet.

I had to stand on the edge of the countertop to reach over and feel for it, but there was a gap between the wall and the cabinet—a sketchbook-wide gap. And into that gap was shoved another black sketchbook like the others. Except this one had been hidden.

It took me a minute to pry it out and then get off the stool and inspect it. It had a title taped to the front. *Why People Take Pictures*. I ran my finger along the black darkroom tape that held the title in place.

It was a weird title.

The implied question seemed as hard to answer as why Darla devoted her short life to making pictures last longer when she, herself, didn't.

Why do people take pictures?

I am no one special

Why People Take Pictures started with a page of scrawl that looked like my own. True story: Darla's handwriting was exactly like mine. Great.

It said:

I am no one special.
    I am tortured by the fact that I am no one special.
    I am comforted by the fact that I am no one special.
    Can you handle that?
    Can you handle that you are most likely no one special too?
    Most people can't handle it.

Shit.
Everything opened up in front of me like a giant railway.

The woman from the mall whose grandson will pass the Fair Pay Act was there. My Irish pig-eating ancestors were there. The mourning dove was there. Ellie was there. Max Black was there, wings like frail, crispy meringue.

This is where the runaway train started down the track. I was inside the dining car enjoying a plate of cookies or something. I didn't feel it then. But the train had been boarded on Saturday night when we drank the bat. And this was the beginning of its journey. Right here.

I am no one special. You are no one special.

Most people can't handle it.

I felt a panic—an urge to run. I remembered that Ellie would soon be on my back porch awaiting commune-contraband lice treatment, so I left the sketchbooks and left the darkroom. When I got upstairs, Dad had accidentally knocked over my shopping bag because I'd left it on the edge of the couch. He found the dress...and the lice treatment.

"Is there something you need to tell me?" he asked, pointing to the box, which he'd left out on the coffee table.

"Ellie's a slut," I said.

He nodded. "Apple doesn't fall far from the tree, then."

Which was the last thing I wanted to hear after reading Darla's crazy notebook.

Jupiterians

I didn't want to see Ellie.

As I waited for her on my back porch, staring out at our barn, I knew I had no logical reason to be mad at her. I didn't know why I was calling her a slut, either. All she did was sleep with Rick, who just happened to have crabs. It was just her bad luck.

"Hey," she said as she came around to the back door.

"Here," I said, handing her the plastic bag with the lice kit in it. I didn't look at her.

"Can I use—um—your barn?"

"Uh."

"Are you seeing weird shit too? Is that why you're not looking at me?"

I looked at her. No transmission. "Seeing what shit?" I stared right into her eyes. Nothing. She stared into mine and I could tell she was disappointed, too.

"I don't know how to describe it. Just weird shit. I was talking to Kyla this morning while we made some trail mix for the party and I looked at her and could see all kinds of strange shit."

I just shrugged as if this wasn't happening to us. As if I didn't have anything to talk about. As if ignoring it would make it go away. I shrugged because I didn't trust Ellie and I didn't want to share a weird accidental superpower with her. I shrugged because so far, shrugging had worked for me in every other weird aspect of my life.

"Hello?"

"What did you see when you looked at her?" I asked.

Ellie frowned. "A bunch of people related to her—like her grandparents or something." She paused. "Maybe I'm just hung over, right?"

"Yeah," I said. "Let's go to the barn."

The barn wasn't like Ellie's barn on the commune. No animals. No hand tools. No lice-infested hippie families moving in or out. It was an artist's studio. It was well lit with skylights on the north side. It still smelled of oil paint even though Dad hadn't painted there for thirteen years.

I flopped myself on the couch and Ellie pulled the lice treatment box from the bag and read the instructions while making a gag face the whole time. "You know what I thought about last night?" she said. "I was looking at the stars and I thought that maybe they're actually Jupiterians."

I looked at her like I didn't follow. Because I didn't follow.

"The lice, I mean. Maybe they're really aliens from Jupiter or another planet and they gather information from human beings by hanging out on their heads or, in this case, in their crotches."

I laughed and shook my head.

"Seriously. Are crotches *not* the most important parts of human beings?"

"I thought you said heads and crotches."

"Exactly. Heads and crotches. The most important parts of human beings," Ellie said.

"So they go from human to human gathering information about what?"

"Everything! I mean, isn't everything they need to know in those two places?"

"Does this mean you aren't going to kill them?" I asked.

"Shit no. I'm killing them right now. I just think it's possible. Right? It's possible that lice are really aliens from some other planet."

"Sure," I said. Anything was possible, even lice-spies from another galaxy.

And though we were both laughing and joking, all we were really thinking about was the transmissions.

"Are we going crazy?" she asked.

I still didn't trust her. I don't know why. It was like some curtain had dropped between us and I couldn't really see her or remember who she was or why we were friends or why I ever liked her. I just wanted to get back to Darla's darkroom.

"Are we?" she asked.

"Maybe the Jupiterians are driving you crazy." I waved her off. "Go kill them. You'll feel better."

She stopped at the bathroom door and said, "I saw Rick with a woman yesterday."

"Shit."

"It was Rachel's mom," she said.

"*Shit,*" I said. "Were they, like, together? Like, *together?*"

"Yeah. I saw them making out through the window of Rachel's RV. The guy is a scumbag."

I said, "He's a scumbag who probably just passed those Jupiterians on to Rachel's mom."

"Who will then pass them on to Rachel's dad."

"Exactly," I said. "I guess it's all one big karmic circle."

"Shit," she said. Then she bit her lip in that way she would when she was thinking hard about something. "Do you think I'm a slut?"

"No!" I said. With an exclamation point. I protested. I exclaimed. I lied.

"I feel like a slut," she said.

"That's bullshit. You slept with one guy."

"A bunch of times."

"So?" I asked.

"While he probably slept with a bunch of other people," she said, her lip quivering a bit. "Well, not probably. I mean— uh—obviously, right?" She held up the box of Jupiterianicide.

"And this makes you a slut how? As I see it, it makes Rick a slut."

"But he's a guy, so that's okay," she said. "And now it's ruined, you know? I should have waited but I didn't and now . . . this!" She shook the box.

"You are not your virginity. You are a human being. The state of your hymen has nothing to do with your worth. Okay? They're fucking with us. They've been fucking with us since the beginning of time."

"Hymen? Shit, Glory. That's deep."

"The world is fucked up," I said. "Go. Get rid of the infiltrators."

She closed the bathroom door and I could hear the water running. She swore and ran a lot of water. I took a picture of the empty box she left on the coffee table. I called it *Be Careful What You Wish For*.

I wondered if I looked at a Jupiterian if I could see its future and its past like I could see the future and the past of the mourning dove and the people at the mall. I wondered if I looked at Jasmine Blue Heffner if I could see Ellie's future.

And why couldn't we see each other? Why was Max Black the bat doing this to us?

Ellie came out of the bathroom walking as if she'd been riding a horse.

"So what did you see?" I asked. "When you looked at Kerry?"

"Kyla."

"Yeah."

"I don't know what I saw. I saw some weird movie in my head—like in my imagination or something."

"You said you saw her grandparents?"

"I don't know who they were. They were related, though. They looked like her. They were dancing. And then I saw Kyla holding a baby. I don't know if it was her baby. She was older. It looked like her baby," Ellie said. She laughed. "It's just the beer, right? I got pretty tanked last night."

"Yeah," I said. "It'll go away."

It was the nineties

Ellie was not a slut. Ellie was my only friend. And I was a loser for thinking all that conflicting shit about her. She went home, Jupiterian free, and told me she'd see me at the star party the following night. I reminded her that I might be late because I had graduation.

This stopped her in midstep. She looked at me and smiled. It was a pained smile.

"I really wish I could be there," she said. "I can't miss your graduation. You're my best friend."

"It's not a big deal. I'll see you at the party. I know they don't want you to—uh—you know."

"Leave?"

"I guess."

"I'll get my dad to stick up for me."

"Good luck with that."

This made us laugh, but without smiling. The kind of laugh that made me realize that Ellie felt left out. That she felt like a freak again. And a slut. And the opposite of free. As I walked back to the house, I thought about what it must be like to be so controlled by Jasmine Blue.

I thought about how controlled I was by a mother who wasn't even there.

Dad was in the kitchen heating up two microwave dinners. Mine had cobbler in the dessert tray and I added a scoop of ice cream because it was delicious. Who wouldn't eat cobbler and ice cream every day if they could? I was no one special and I could eat cobbler and ice cream every fucking day if I wanted.

When dinner was done, we tossed our plastic trays into the recycling and Dad went back to the couch and his laptop while I made a move toward the basement door.

"Find anything interesting down there today?" Dad asked.

I wanted to tell him about Darla's hidden sketchbook. Instead, I asked, "What did you mean when you said Ellie didn't fall far from the tree? I take it Jasmine Blue was—uh...?"

"It was the nineties."

"It wasn't that different."

"It was different when we all moved out here," he said.

"So she was a slut, then? That's what you said, right?"

"Jasmine Blue did her own thing. Still does." He laughed.

"Ellie isn't really a slut. She just had a boyfriend," I said. "Who was a dick."

"I'm glad it was that stuff and not a pregnancy test. For her sake, I mean."

"Yeah."

He worked on his computer while we talked. I don't think I ever just saw him doing one thing. Could never slow his brain down enough to meditate, I bet. Maybe that was why he and Darla stopped hanging out at the commune.

"So? Was it good down there?" he asked again.

"I can't wait to start working," I said. "I have a roll of black-and-white to develop and then I'll get some cheap paper and remember how to print. It's been a while since Mr. Wilson's history of photography class."

"Ugh!" He said it with that exclamation point. *Ugh!* As if I'd just lanced a boil right in front of him or something.

"What?"

"Don't buy cheap paper. Leave that to me. I'll order it online. Trust me."

"But—I—"

"There's new developer and fixer already. I put it under the kitchen sink."

"Oh." How did he know I needed it?

"We used to spend hours in there together."

"You must miss her," I said. I don't know why I said it. Except that maybe it was true. And the truth *is.*

He sighed. "Every single day, Cupcake. Every single day." He smiled and looked at me and I avoided eye contact by looking at his arm. "And you're graduating tomorrow," he said. "And time just flew by."

Sounds so convenient, right? Me not having a mom and my dad being all great about it and stuff. But it wasn't like that. The air was tense. We still had no oven. My cobbler still tasted like radiation, no matter how much ice cream I piled onto it. I could feel the secrets in the soil here. The way Dad talked about Jasmine Blue and the nineties. Something was about to sprout and grow from that soil. I could feel it the same as I could see the mourning dove into infinity.

BOOK TWO

The consequence of the bat

Graduation day means you must now do something with your life. You must grow up and buy your own train tickets, accrue student debt so you can become part of the machine. You must pick a major. The light comes only after that. Sorry about saying that graduation is the light at the end of the tunnel. That was a lie.

The world is never what it seems

The day of graduation, the mourning dove didn't sit where I could see it. I could hear it. I could always hear it. *Twooooeee-toooo-tooo-tooo.* But I couldn't see it to test my magical bat powers. I was partly relieved because I didn't really *want* to have magical bat powers. I was hoping all of that was left in yesterday—that sleep had cured me.

I snuck down to the darkroom first thing, while Dad was in the bathroom doing his usual morning routine. I opened *Why People Take Pictures* to the next random page of scribble. There weren't many of them. Mostly, it was pictures with handwritten captions, just like my sketchbooks.

The page read:

I am tortured by the mundane. You are mundane. I am tortured by you.

I am tortured by eating, drinking, and sleeping. I am tortured by brushing my teeth. I am tortured by the dishes that are always in the sink even though I do them four times a day. I am tortured by basmati rice, by egg noodles, by goddamn boneless chicken breasts. I am tortured by beef bouillon and salt and pepper. I am tortured by lunch foods. Limited options. Ham and cheese. Peanut butter and jelly. Soup and sandwich. Salads.

     Is this okay? Are you all right? Are you tortured too?

Shit.

Shit. Shit. Shit.

I read it three more times. I asked myself the question. *Are you tortured too?*

Are you?

I pulled out my own sketchbook and I wrote the answer.

I am tortured too. I am tortured by belly fat and magazine covers about how to please everyone but myself. I am tortured by sheep who click on anything that will guarantee a ten-pound loss in one week. Sheep who will get on their knees if it means someone will like them more.

     I am tortured by my inability to want to hang out with desperate people. I am tortured by goddamned yearbooks full of bullshit. I met you when. I'll miss the times. I'll keep in touch. Best friends forever.

     Is this okay? Are you all right? Are you tortured too?

I had to be at the school for graduation by eleven, so I didn't have time to read or write any more. I didn't feel like going to graduation. I didn't feel like doing any of it. Not the cap and gown. Not the swishy tassel with the brass '14. Not the line of congratulatory teachers. I wanted to just sit there and read Darla's *Why People Take Pictures* all day.

Because I *was* tortured.

By questions whose answers might live inside her book.

By the elephants living all over my house. (Hint: Check the freezer.)

By lunch foods, too. I hated sandwiches and salads and everything lunchy. When I read that part, I felt like someone might finally understand me. But maybe hating lunch foods was another step toward...you know.

I turned the page and found a picture of a naked woman, the photo torn right across her shoulders. It wasn't like the stuff Markus Glenn showed me on his laptop in seventh grade. It wasn't like any picture Darla ever took. It was in color. It was soft focused. Warmly toned. The backdrop was wrinkled and too close to the woman. The lighting was harsh and cast deep shadows.

Above the picture Darla wrote: *Why would anyone do this?*

Under the picture Darla wrote: *The world is never what it seems.*

I turned to the next page not really prepared for what was coming.

It was a portrait of a man with no head because he had shot it off with the gun that was still lying next to him on the bed.

Above the picture Darla wrote: *Why would anyone do this?*

Under the picture Darla wrote: *I've decided to name him Bill.*

I stared at the picture for a long time.

"Bill" had his jaw, a tiny portion of his ear, and his beard. That was really all that was left of his head. His jaw was blown out, it was twice as wide as it should have been and the ear and the sideburn connecting the two, they were sticky and brown and swollen, as if the head was trying to make up for the lack of itself. As if it was trying to fill in the missing pieces that were scattered all over the room. His flannel shirt looked new and as if it had been ironed that morning. It was black with his blood, but I could see the flannel pattern under the wetness.

He looked like a big man. With his head, I'd say he was over six feet. Maybe six foot one or two. By his side there was a shotgun of some kind. I didn't know guns. We were peaceful out here in nonconsumerist artist/hippie weirdo freak land. We didn't even lock our doors.

I looked back at the picture of the naked woman with her head torn off. It had the same question as the picture of Bill. *Why would anyone do this?*

I braced myself for the contents of the next page, but all it was, was the chemical backstory of stop bath. Stop bath is the acid that stops a silver gelatin print from developing in developer. The order of simple printing is: Developer, stop bath, fixer, rinse. When you put an exposed piece of paper into (alkaline) developer, it will continue to develop until you put it into (acid) stop bath.

Darla's desired working stop bath was 0.85% acetic acid.

Apparently, Darla was into the history of acetic acid. I found it boring and would be late for graduation if I didn't get back upstairs, get showered and get dressed, so I closed the book and put it back in its hiding place. But I couldn't get Bill out of my head. And it turned out Darla couldn't either.

If there was a stop bath—an emotional sort of stop bath for thoughts like that—would Darla be alive today? And if so, what was that stop bath?

————

After a shower and some forced relaxation yoga that didn't do much but make me feel like a failure at yoga and relaxing, I went downstairs and flopped myself next to Dad, who was working on his laptop on the couch trying to help three online chat customers at one time. I stared at the screen and avoided eye contact, which was easy from that position.

"This one doesn't even know what the word *reboot* means," he said. "There should be a test before you're allowed to buy a computer."

I looked at him as he typed and then clicked and then typed again. He was handsome. Rugged. Smart. So smart. Smart enough to know that he shouldn't be on the couch dealing with people who didn't know what *reboot* meant.

"Ellie called," he said. "She'll meet you at the school."

"Oh," I said. "Did you offer her a ride?"

"Yeah. She said she had one."

I looked up at the painting on the wall. *Woman.* I looked at her curves, her plain face, her pale skin, her relaxed pose. I looked back at Dad typing on the couch. I thought about Darla's pictures. The woman with no head. The man with no head. I tried to figure out what it meant. I wanted to ask Dad where Darla got the picture of the dead guy, Bill. I wanted to ask if Darla was some crime scene photographer or something. I wanted to know where she got the naked picture of the now-headless woman.

But it was graduation day. I didn't want to ruin it. So, I said something I'd been meaning to say to Dad since the ninth grade, which was the last time I'd said it.

"Dad?" I asked.

"Yeah," he said, still typing something.

"I want you to paint again."

"Uh-huh."

"No. I mean it."

"You going to pay the bills?" he asked.

"The trust will pay the bills and you know it."

That was true. We owned the house. We didn't buy much. We barely used our phones. And the trust was large last time I peeked at the bank statement that I wasn't supposed to be peeking at.

I pointed to Mom's pictures. "See that wall?" A series of landscapes I never really liked. They were dull. I didn't care how long they'd last, how every zone was represented, or how meticulously she'd framed them. Who gives a shit about a tree stump and a triptych of large rocks? "I want a Roy O'Brien on that wall. Something that screams at me. I want that." I didn't tell him about the German expressionist oven paintings in my head.

"I have to get back to work," he said.

Free yourself. Have the courage.

"What happened to you?" I asked Ellie. She'd been standing by herself in the school parking lot and once I parked, she came to my driver's-side door the minute I got out of the car. She had things written up and down her forearms in black Sharpie marker. Her hair was wet with sweat, and there was some sort of debris in it.

"I don't think I can stay," she said, blinking a lot and looking mostly at the macadam under our feet in the school's back parking lot.

I held my gown, sheathed in thin dry cleaner's plastic, over my left arm, and I reached out to her with my right.

"This has been the most fucked-up day of my life," she said.

"Are you okay? Did something happen?" I asked. She looked almost beat up.

"I'm fine," she said.

"What's that?" I asked, and pointed to her arms.

She ignored my question and said, "I saw so many things today, Glory. Weird things."

"I know. I see it too, remember? It's cool."

"It's not cool!" she yelled. "It's not cool!"

"What did you see?"

"*Everything*. People having sex or people dying or people being born or . . . I don't know. Weird things."

"Like the future?"

"Yeah."

"But you can't see mine, right?"

She looked right into my eyes. "No."

"How did you get here?" I asked.

"I walked."

We lived over four miles away. "You walked?"

She put her arms out in a shrug. I could read what she'd written inside her left forearm. *Free yourself. Have the courage.*

"I don't know what to do with this—this stuff I'm seeing. I'm not sure what any of it means."

"Maybe it doesn't mean anything," I said.

"It means something. I know it." She looked at the message written up her arms and I had this feeling like it wasn't a message meant for her—that maybe it was a message meant for me.

"I have to go," I said.

She nodded.

"Just don't look at people. That's the key. We'll talk later," I said.

She nodded again. Quickly. Like she was high or something.

She walked away through a sea of cars. I walked toward the gym.

Transmission from Jody Heckman, lead majorette and president of the student council: *Her great-grandmother was assaulted by twelve soldiers in Nazi Germany. Her great-granddaughter will suffer the same fate in the Second US Civil War.*

I looked away.

Second Civil War?

I slipped on my white gown and I secured my cap with two bobby pins that I got from the giant tub of bobby pins on the front table. Then I filed into my alphabetical place between Jason Oberholtzer and Ron Oliveli and stood there looking at the linoleum tiles in a weird sort of limbo.

I thought about Darla's darkroom. I thought about the pictures I would develop and print that summer. I thought about the way everything has stages. My relationship with Dad. My relationship with Ellie. My relationship with this day: graduation day.

It was all like developing pictures: Developer, stop bath, fixer, rinse.

There are stages.

There is a moment in every photograph's life when it has been exposed but not developed. The light from the enlarger has shone through the negative and made its impression on the paper, but without the magic of developer, the paper will stay white and no one will ever see what that impression is.

Standing in the cafeteria between Jason and Ron, I felt

like that piece of paper. Exposed but not developed. Potential beneath the surface. Blank.

At the same time, I knew if I looked up and met eyes with any of my classmates, I would learn more about them than any of them would ever know about themselves. I both wanted to do it and didn't want to do it. I thought about the possibility of a second civil war and decided to browse the graduation program instead.

It wasn't until we started to walk toward the football stadium single file that I realized that most everyone is just like me—exposed but not developed. Secretive. Scared. I decided I should dunk the audience in psychic developer and see whatever the bat wanted me to see.

Transmission from Mrs. Lingle, the school secretary: *Her father used to play tennis every day until he had to get his knee replaced and now he feels useless.*

Transmission from Mr. Knapp, the shop teacher: *His granddaughter will play piano in Carnegie Hall. She will feel like an utter failure, regardless.*

Transmission from Dad, who stood at the stairs as we descended them toward the stage that was assembled in the grass of the football field: *His grandfather used to call him Roy the Boy because he was the only boy out of twenty cousins. His mother often thought being the only boy made him spoiled, so she tried to withhold any outward signs of affection for as long as she could until she finally left and never came back.*

Transmission from a random parent who snapped pictures from the sidelines: *Her mother is dying in a nursing home across town. Her mother was a nurse who worked to heal patients from radiation poisoning in Japan in 1945 after the US dropped an atomic bomb on Hiroshima. The bomb was named Little Boy.*

I looked down.

All the way to the aisle, to my row, and then to my seat, I looked down.

Who would name a 9,700-pound bomb *Little Boy*, anyway?

The bat wanted me to ask that. It showed me what it wanted to show me. It showed me what it knew I wanted to see. Why did it want me to see so much pain? Why couldn't I see anything warm and fuzzy and emotionally sweet? I wanted to see everything, now. I wanted to see everything.

I would fly

Graduation was an endurance test. Kids got diplomas, shook hands with the superintendent and handed him a lollipop secretly as a joke. His pockets bulged after forty of them. We had a class of 343. He had to start emptying into the podium every few rows. I did not grab a lollipop when I was leaving the cafeteria. I was not going to play a joke on the superintendent.

Gerald Faust, our resident reality TV star, accepted his diploma with Native American war paint on his face. He pushed a girl I never saw before in a wheelchair up a makeshift plywood ramp on the left side. She gave the superintendent a lollipop.

At one point during the endless wait to get past the *M* names, I met eyes with a kid standing in the aisle waiting to go to the stage. I'd never seen him before. He had the most beautiful brown eyes.

Transmission from Beautiful Brown Eyes: *His grandfather*

escaped Cuba in the 1960s and lived long enough to see this day. His grandfather's grandfather was killed in the Partido Independiente de Color in 1912, fighting for the rights of Afro-Cubans. His grandson will also die fighting for rights in the Second Civil War.

I smiled shyly at the beautiful brown-eyed kid and then looked down at my program. I paged through the list of 343 graduates. Some had asterisks behind their names. Some didn't. If I let my eyes go lazy, all the type blurred into one big block of blue ink.

I am no one special. You are no one special. Can you handle that? Most people can't handle it.

I am tortured by the mundane. You are mundane. I am tortured by you.

I looked down at my Doc Martens shoes. I'd shined them and bought new white bobby socks. No one could see my dress under the gown, but I felt it there, a size too big, making me smaller, shrinking me into the size of a bat.

When it was finally time for our row to go up, I stood and smoothed out my gown and took a deep breath. I thought of Darla. I pictured Bill, the man with no head. I pictured the headless naked body from the previous page in Darla's book. *Why would anyone do this?*

I thought of Letter *N* Day. I thought about how my formal education started there, on that day, and how it was going to end today. From now on, I wasn't going to keep my life a secret. I was going to be a natural human being, if there was such a thing. I was going to be free. Life, liberty and don't tread on me. I would fly.

Maybe this is what *Free yourself. Have the courage* meant.

After this stupid ceremony, I would talk about it. Darla. Suicide. Whatever would help me move forward. Whatever made me stop thinking I was doomed. I was not doomed. Was I? I was not another apple who would fall too close to the tree. Was I?

I said this in my head, but underneath it all were chemistry and genes and questions that had never been answered. Questions I had never asked.

———

We were fed onto the stage like machine parts. We were a conveyor belt of future. We were an assembly line of tomorrow. We were handed our diplomas and stood to face the audience and they were asked not to clap until the end, but some did anyway.

I heard Dad yell. "Cupcake!"

I heard Ellie, from somewhere. "Hell yeah!"

I smiled and looked at the superintendent. *His distant descendant will die in the twenty-fourth century's World War IV, because his brothers will close the shelter door and leave him out. True story: Radiation poisoning decreases the faster you get into a shelter. Even if you lock out your own brother.*

I stood and faced the crowd and heard a static of epic proportions. Chatter of a thousand infinities all at once. I saw cavemen and space stations. I saw wars fought on horseback and wars fought with photon torpedoes. I looked back down, exited via the steps to the right and took my place on the assembly line. We filed back to our row and shimmied into our places and sat down on cue.

Like dogs.

Like well-trained dogs.

We were halfway through the *W* names when I saw Ellie walking behind the away bleachers. The away bleachers were empty because they were behind the stage. She found a place in the shade under the middle of the bleachers and sat down. Then she stood up and drew something on the bottom side of the bleacher seats, one after the other.

I watched her all the way through to Deanna Zwicky and then the Class of 2014 was instructed to stand and move our tassels from one side to the other and we were reminded for the tenth time not to throw our caps because our mortarboards could take an eye out.

Max Black the bat showed me how we were obedient monkeys. He told me to guess what Ellie was writing under the bleachers.

Free yourself. Have the courage.

Which was a fine thing to do if you were no one special.

I looked at the backs of three-hundred-plus heads and thought: *What a perfect day to figure this out.*

If Max Black the bat had had full control, I'd have stood on my folding chair right then and screamed it. I'd have rushed the stage and chanted it into the microphone. I'd have outdone all those bullshit speeches I heard that day.

My speech would have been about the nature of us.

Human beings.

How we're a pack of self-centered animals.

I'd have named my speech: *You are mundane.*

Pay to the order of

"Did you hear me yell?" Dad asked.

"All those years to plan what you're going to yell at my graduation and you chose *Cupcake*," I said, hugging him.

He gave me a card.

"For now or later?" I asked. We met eyes. Transmission from Dad: *An ancestor of his once killed a man over a hard-boiled egg. His wife was pregnant and hungry. She had a girl.*

"Either. But if you open it now, it might make you smile."

Only when he said that did I realize I hadn't been smiling. Not sure for how long. Maybe thirteen years. I made sure to draw up the sides of my mouth and I slipped my finger into the sky-blue envelope and ripped it across the top seam.

For My Graduate...

There was a black-and-white photograph of a graduate on the front and inside there was a check for fifty thousand dollars.

I snapped the card shut the minute I saw the amount scrawled out on the line below PAY TO THE ORDER OF. Then I opened it again and peeked. It still said fifty thousand dollars.

"Oh my God," I said.

Dad pulled me into his side and hugged me and kissed me on the head.

I didn't know what to do.

I took the card and put it in the large square pocket of my Dust Bowl dress and I hugged Dad and then I hugged him more and then I worried about what I would blow fifty thousand dollars on and then I stopped worrying and then I looked over Dad's shoulder and I met eyes with someone's grandmother.

Transmission from a random grandmother: *Her great-grandson will leave and never talk to the family again... and will eventually find the loophole in the Fair Pay Act. And that loophole will open a whole can of insanity.*

"It's too much," I said to Dad. "I can't keep it."

"You can and you will so keep it. Your mother wanted you to have it. You didn't know her, but I can tell you: You never go against your mother."

I wanted to say: *Or she'll stick her head in the oven and make you live on radiated food for the rest of your life.*

Instead, I just touched the card through the stiff seer-sucker. Instead, I felt like throwing up because being cynical wasn't working. My mother was dead. She had been dead for thirteen years and it was sad. Not just for me, but for Dad. I hugged him again and it was a real hug—no pats on the back or jokes. He hugged me the same way. It was our first real hug as adults or something.

"We need to talk more about stuff," I said into his ear.

"Okay," he answered.

"I'm a little lost, but I think I'll be okay," I said. Then I pulled back and looked into his eyes.

Transmission from Dad: *His sisters didn't call him much. His friends didn't call him much.*

I tried to see his future. My future. Anything that would back up that stupid shit I just said about being lost, but being okay. But there was no future when I looked at him.

"I think that check might help you see your options," he said.

I looked around to other graduates and their parents and I doubted any of them were walking around with fifty thousand dollars and knowledge of a second civil war in their pockets. I doubted any of them had an intense feeling like they could just die any minute.

The crowd of graduates and relatives let out random screams of joy or relief or football team camaraderie. People tried to move through and Dad and I were constantly being separated by people who said, "Can I cut through here?"

It was as if all the other families were too strong to cut through, but ours had an expressway.

"Do you mind if I get out of here?" Dad asked after about four minutes.

"Nah."

"Not my scene, you know?" He meant people. People were not his scene.

"I'm going soon, too," I said. "Just after I return my stuff. I'll be home later."

I stood there still denying I had fifty grand in my pocket and looked around. I tried to see Ellie, but she wasn't there. Too many people stood between me and the away bleachers, in case she was still there.

I still had the bat-vision. I didn't like the transmissions, but I wanted to find out more. The next civil war. The future of our galaxy. The horror of our past.

I popped in and out of people's infinities. I asked Max Black the bat if he could show me something funny or nice for once.

Her father knew John F. Kennedy.

His great-granduncle was a politician and helped end local prohibition.

His distant descendant will be the interior designer for Earth's first orbiter, the station called Lincoln. *He will misspell* Lincoln *on the blueprints by leaving out the second* L.

Her grandson will discover the gene that causes stupidity and will be jailed for suggesting that it be eliminated.

His grandniece will give birth to a man called Nedrick the Sanctimonious who will start the Second Civil War, which will split our country in two: the New America, where Nedrick will rule through his cronies in political office and his stockpile of weapons sent from dubious worldwide militias to help destroy the most powerful country on Earth, and the Old America, which will gain support from most of the world because it is horrifying to watch a potentially great country move backward. And because sanctimony is annoying.

A second civil war? What could bring us there again?

As I looked from person to person and learned more about the wider details, I felt all-powerful and yet helpless. I had knowledge. Maybe.

Or maybe I was nuts. 50% Darla. A bat. God.

Whatever was going on, I decided there in the packed, humid parking lot that I would use my transmissions to write the history of the future.

Can you believe it, Glory?

The history of the future had an ending just like our beginning. I saw that when I looked at Jupiter two nights before.

The history of the future started with a huge explosion that made Little Boy, the 9,700-pound atomic bomb that was not a microwave oven or a cell phone, look like a microwave oven or a cell phone. Call it the big bang; call it what you want. We are all made from star dust and we will all return to star dust, like a cosmic palindrome.

We are birthed and we are ended.

We are all potentially bat dust in pickle jars. Mixed with beer, we could cause hallucinations and the urge to write on ourselves with Sharpie markers.

The history of the future would have to be written in a way unlike my other sketchbooks. It would sort through the static I was seeing and would pull out the important facts. It would be something people in the future could read so they might understand what will happen.

Before I could get out of the cafeteria, Stacy Cullen came up to me and hugged me as if we were best friends. Stacy and I were in first grade together. Now we graduated together. She had tears in her eyes.

"Can you believe it, Glory?"

I stared at her. Her transmission was horrifying.

"I know, right? I don't know what to say, either," she said. "It's all so amazing."

"Yeah," I said. "Amazing."

"Next thing you know we'll be graduating from college and all married and shit."

"Sure," I said, not taking my eyes off her infinity.

She stopped and looked embarrassed. "Sorry," she said.

I had no idea what she could be sorry about. I was far sorrier for her.

Transmission from Stacy: *Her oldest son will die instantly in a head-on collision with a drunk driver who will pass out at the wheel on Route 422. It will be summertime. Her two younger sons will never get over it. The youngest will move to Idaho and never come home. The middle boy will give her two grand-daughters, who will be stolen during the Second Civil War, which will be common practice during the reign of Nedrick the Sancti-monious.*

"I'm really sorry, Glory," she said again.

"No problem, really," I said, so sad for her granddaughters.

"I didn't mean to rub it in your face," she said.

That's when I realized she was talking about college. I guess that's what normal, not-God-drinking people think about at graduation. Future. College. Marriage. Adulthood.

"You totally didn't rub it in my face," I said. Then I felt the fifty thousand dollars in my pocket. "I just want to take a year off to get my shit together. That's all."

She nodded nervously, looking past me to the door. "Okay. Well, good luck!" Another hug. Then she left.

I was left standing there looking at the throng of other graduates returning their gowns, thinking about college, futures, marriage, adulthood. They all looked happy about being on the conveyor belt of life. They didn't know anything about the Second Civil War.

Glory O'Brien's History of the Future

I am Glory O'Brien and I am writing this book because something is going to happen. Something bad.

I know things. I can't tell you how I know things, but I know things and I am writing them down here in case anyone ever wants to know what I know. The year is 2014. The bad things will happen in about fifty years or so.

From what I can see, and I can't see everything, it will all start with the Fair Pay Act...or more accurately, the loophole someone will find in order to avoid it.

The Fair Pay Act will be a federal law that will finally require employers to pay women the same as men for performing the same jobs. It, or something like it, has been on the minds of some law-makers since the late twentieth century but never quite evened out the pay situation.

The loophole in the federal Fair Pay Act will be simple.

How can states make sure they won't have to pay women fairly?

Make it illegal for women to work.

Genius.

It will take one short month for the first state legislature to exploit the loophole in the Fair Pay Act and to pass the Family Protection Act.

A week later, when the governor gives it his stamp of approval, women representatives and senators will be escorted out of their offices and will be given no opportunity to appeal.

It will, from that day forward, be illegal for them to work in their own state. Even as a waitress. Even as a lap dancer. Even as an Avon makeup representative.

The governor will call this a victory for families.

Most people can't handle it

Ellie was in my car. I had no idea how she got there, because I'd locked it. She still looked like she was losing her mind, evident by the fact that she was sitting in my car in the hot parking lot with the windows up. It had to be a hundred degrees in there, easily.

I opened the door and sat in the driver's seat. "Hi."

"I want it to go away," she said.

"I'm seeing a civil war. And other stuff. Today I saw an intergalactic war with photon torpedoes. I think it's kinda cool."

"I'm seeing things I don't care about."

"Like?"

"Naked people."

"Naked people?"

I looked at Ellie then and noticed that she'd worn her

favorite sundress but she'd left the buttons in the front open. And she wasn't wearing a bra. Come to think of it, I don't know if anyone on the commune wore a bra. Maybe bras were like atomic bombs, too.

I looked down at my seersucker Dust Bowl dress and bobby socks. I knew I couldn't compete, but I never wanted to compete. I liked how white my legs were. I planned on keeping them sun free by spending my entire summer in the darkroom becoming Darla. I didn't remember Darla's legs, but I'd seen pictures, and in them her legs were white too. She had knobby knees.

Only there, on graduation day in the car with Ellie, did I realize I had knobby knees too.

When I thought about it, no one I ever saw on TV or in a magazine or on a billboard had knobby white knees or a Dust Bowl dress.

"What are we going to do?" Ellie asked. "I can't just avoid people for the rest of my life."

Of course, I could. I totally *could* avoid people for the rest of my life. "Just chill out. We'll be fine. Everything is happening for a reason."

"We're going crazy for a reason? What the fuck? I got fucking crabs off some asshole for a reason? I'm nearly eighteen and I don't have a high school diploma for a *reason*?"

I put the car in reverse. "Okay, if you can't chill out then just shut up. Or maybe say *congratulations* or something appropriate. Or just something not insane," I said. "Because you're not insane, you know. I see it too, okay? You're not anything special."

She looked hurt. "I'm not anything special?"

"I am no one special. You are no one special. Can you handle that?" I said. "Most people can't handle it."

"Shit," she said.

Then I backed out of the parking space, drove to the parking lot's exit and got stuck in the dumb postceremony traffic jam that had built up while I was making small talk with Stacy Cullen. I wished I'd left with Dad, who was surely home by now in a tie-dyed shirt and a pair of baggy pajama shorts on the couch with his laptop.

"Congratulations," she said, finally.

"Thanks." I thought about how Ellie wasn't going to be my friend soon. How I'd planned to get away from her somehow. How she didn't know my biggest secret—about becoming Darla.

I pointed to her arms. "Where'd you get that idea?" I asked. "Free yourself, have the courage?"

"I don't know," she said. "The bat gave it to me. Saturday night, remember?"

We let silence fall between us for a minute.

After a while, she said, "We should tell someone."

"No one would believe us if we told them." I put the car in park and waited for traffic. I grabbed my camera and took a picture of Ellie's arms. I'd call it: *The Consequence of the Bat*.

Once I pulled out of the traffic and onto the small highway that would get us home, Ellie started with small talk and I started to compile a timeline in my head. If Stacy Cullen's granddaughters would be sacrificed in the Second Civil War, then that would happen around the late twenty-first century or so, depending on when people have kids, I guessed. They looked young, like most parents did in the transmissions— like all those old pictures from the East where daughters are sold as teenagers to men. That's what it looked like.

It scared me and yet it seemed like a worthy project or something—to document it, even if it was some hallucinatory reaction to the bat. What else did I have to do?

Before Max Black, the future seemed boring and there wasn't much to think about. After Max Black, it was like I was looking at a negative, a stack of photographic paper, a jar full of emulsion, a paintbrush, and trays full of chemistry. There was now so much to do.

So much to do.

I couldn't think of a title

When we got home, Ellie went to her house and I told her I'd see her later at the star party. Dad was in place on the couch, laptop stuck to his knees, and he said a bunch of cheery stuff to me as I went upstairs to change. I looked at myself in my seersucker dress one last time before I took it off. I slipped the fifty thousand dollars out of the pocket and put the card and the check on my desk.

I stared at it.

I looked at the numbers. 5, 0, 0, 0, 0. I took a picture of it, but I couldn't think of a title.

This was Darla's graduation present for me.

I didn't think the obvious things here. I didn't think about how I'd rather have her than money. I didn't think that this could buy me a new future or some path that made some sort of sense to a high school guidance counselor.

Anyway, Darla left me a lot more than a dumb fifty thousand dollars. She left me her sketchbooks. Her darkroom. Her cameras. Her knees. Her hair. Could fifty thousand dollars buy my way out of following in her footsteps? I had no idea. Because I still didn't know why she took those footsteps.

I put on a pair of old jeans and a T-shirt and flopped back downstairs so I could get back to *Why People Take Pictures*.

"I'm going to Ellie's star party tonight, okay?" I said.

"Sure thing." Then Dad looked up at me. "Shit, Cupcake. Should I have asked if you wanted a graduation party? Crap. I never even thought of that."

"Nah. Who would I invite?"

"Friends? Family?"

"So Aunt Amy could come over and try to tell me about the Virgin Mary again? Yeah. That would have been comfortable."

"True," he said. "But Ellie's mom shouldn't be the one throwing you a party."

"She's not throwing *me* a party. She's throwing the *stars* a party. I just get to crash," I said. "Anyway. Until then, I'm printing." I waved and walked toward the basement door. He didn't stop me. He didn't ask me what I was printing. He didn't point out that I didn't have new paper yet. He didn't point out that I probably wasn't printing. He didn't point out that I couldn't *really* become Darla, even if I wanted to. Even if I took over her quest for the everlasting print. Even if I wore Dorothea Lange Dust Bowl dresses every day. Even if I stuck my head in the microwave and turned my head into Hiroshima.

I retrieved and opened up *Why People Take Pictures* and paged directly to Bill, the man with no head. I stared at his exposed connective tissue and broken bones. Every color you could think of was there. Different shades of yellow—fat cells, bone particles, tendons, parts of teeth. Oranges and reds and deep purples and blues. A rainbow of death. All that color, but still no head. Just a neck and part of a jaw. All that color and still max black for Bill. Nothing. Zero. No more anything for Bill.

Could I ever really wish this on myself? I liked my knobby knees. My dumb Irish nose. Why was I looking at this? Why was Darla?

I turned the page and there were four black-and-white pictures of a tooth. A pulled tooth—the whole thing, long, curved roots and all—lying on different backgrounds. The first background was white, which made the tooth look several shades of gray. The second background was a bunch of pebbles, and the tooth was barely visible in the chaos, but when it popped, it was particularly creepy. The third background was dirt. Darla had built a 6-inch-high mound of dirt and laid the tooth right on top like an offering on an altar, and the focus was the tooth, with the dirt beyond it fading into blurry nothingness. The fourth background was black and the stark contrast between the tooth and the black made the texture of the tooth more obvious. Ridges and burrs and layers of enamel all wrapped into one dead tooth. Who knew a tooth had so much texture? So much life—even though it was dead?

She drew an arrow to that picture, the fourth one, and

wrote: *Max Black and #46.* She drew a frowny face next to it like this. ☹

Then she wrote: *Now #46 and Bill can go preserve peaches with my mom.*

My mother had clearly gone bonkers.

This is why she stuck her head in the oven rather than making perfectly *N*-shaped Rice Krispies Treats for my pre-school class thirteen years ago. This is why she chose to concentrate more on making pictures last longer rather than herself.

I wanted an answer. That had to be the answer. *Now #46 and Bill can go preserve peaches with my mom.*

I turned the page and found three more naked pictures of what looked like the same photo shoot from the first naked picture. This time the head wasn't ripped off, though.

This time, the head was there in full view.

And it was Jasmine Blue Heffner's head.

The creepiest thing about this was that young Jasmine Blue looked exactly like Ellie in the pictures. It was like looking at a naked picture of Ellie and it felt twenty shades of not right.

We are all naked under our clothes.

What does she have that's so special?

Ripping meat from the bone

Going to the star party that night took on a whole new light after I found those pictures. How would I ever look Jasmine Blue Heffner in the face again?

I wanted to read the whole book right then—call off going to Ellie's and stay in the darkroom until I was done—but then I looked back at those pictures of Jasmine Blue and I closed the book.

If Darla's question was *Why do people take pictures?*, then what sort of answer was that? Or were pictures like that why Darla was asking in the first place?

I said, to the empty room, "I take pictures because sometimes I can't find the words to say what I want to say."

There was no answer, but I felt as if I was haunted—as if I heard someone breathe right there next to me. It sounds stupid now, but I was scared. Maybe Bill was there. Maybe Darla was. I saw something move—something translucent.

I put *Why People Take Pictures* behind the cabinet and I locked the darkroom door. I went upstairs two steps at a time and closed the basement door the minute I got upstairs.

"Dad?"

He looked up. Transmission from Dad: *An ancestor brick-layer from the nineteenth century stood on the top of a tall city building, smiling and taking in the view.*

"Can we talk about something?" I asked.

He must have noticed the seriousness of my tone because he put his computer on the coffee table and sat up. "Sure. What's up?" he asked.

"It's about Jasmine Blue," I said. "And why you don't talk to her."

A lot of awkward silence here.

Oh well.

I said, "You knew each other before, right?"

"We all moved out here together...technically. The four of us." I stayed quiet. He added, "Me, your mom, Jasmine and Ed."

"And?"

"We had big ideas."

"Like?"

He sighed and shook his head. "We were going to start a nonconsumerist movement. Drop out. No attachment. No stuff," he said. "We were stupid kids."

I didn't say anything, but I didn't think that was a particularly stupid-kid way of thinking...unless that made me a stupid kid, which was probably up for debate considering my recent two-steps-at-a-time escape from my own basement, not to mention my lack of future plans.

He said, "The eighties and nineties were so... full of *stuff.* Materialistic. Everybody wanted a shiny new car. Money trees. Suits and ties. Everybody was greedy, you know?"

I nodded, but I didn't know why this was so different from now. That was what everyone at graduation wanted. Success. Spell that with dollar signs. $UCCE$$.

"So what happened?" I asked.

"Jasmine started gathering her flock."

"Which means?"

"She invited other people to start living over there. People who agreed with everything she said," he said.

"So all those people weren't there in the beginning?"

"No."

"Did they drop you guys when new people showed up or something?"

"Not quite."

"So, what's the big deal? It's their house. They can have people live there if they want, right?"

"It's been a long time," he said.

"Are you saying you can't remember? Because I don't believe you."

"No. It's just—complicated."

"I don't know. I can understand what it's like when your best friend gets new friends. That must hurt."

"Yeah. That's not quite how it went," he said.

"Well, yeah. The new friends moved onto Jasmine's farm and started the commune without you, but right across the road. Is that close?"

He pointed toward the commune. "That," he said. "That...
place...isn't Jasmine's."

"Oh," I said. "Whose is it?"

"It was given to her. By your mother," he said. *"Given."*

"Given?"

"Well, maybe more like borrowed."

"Like, she didn't sell it to her? She just...what? Said, *Hey you can live here*?"

"Yep."

"Huh," I said. "So...Jasmine stopped talking to you guys once you gave her a house to live in?"

"Kinda," he said.

"But she and Mom were close once, right?"

"Best friends."

"And then...they weren't?"

He sighed again. "Shit, Cupcake. It's a hell of a long story."

"And I really want to know," I said.

"It's adult stuff. I mean—I know you're old enough, but you're still my kid," he said. "It's not the kind of stuff you tell your kid."

"I might already know more than you think I know. So you should tell me the rest or else you'll die one day and I'll never know the truth and that would suck."

He stared at me.

I said, "What did Jasmine do?"

"Uh—she—uh. She didn't—uh—something—uh..."

"Seriously? You can't tell me?"

He exhaled. "Jasmine tried to steal me away from your mother," he said. "She tried really hard."

He made a face then. Like he'd just eaten a bad piece of shellfish. "I didn't handle it right," he went on, before I had a chance to say anything. "Darla had every reason to be angry."

"Is that why . . . ?"

"No."

"It didn't have anything to do with it?"

"No."

"So she and Jasmine had a big fight or something?"

I felt bad for pressing. But at the same time, I'd just found naked pictures of Jasmine Blue Heffner in a secret book in Darla's darkroom and I wanted to know where they came from.

He was quiet and sent out signals that the conversation was over.

I didn't want to piss Dad off and then leave.

I didn't want to make him sad, either.

But I was inexplicably angry about those pictures.

He put the laptop back on his lap and started to type as if we weren't having a conversation and that made me angry. The old, not-graduated Glory O'Brien might have just microwaved a snack pocket cherry pie, but Glory O'Brien the bat wanted the truth. I stood with my hand on my hip.

"Did Mom take those pictures of her? Is that one of those weird nineties things you talk about? Posing naked and stuff like that?"

It took a minute for my question to prance across the room and into his ears, but once it did, he put his face into his hands. For a second I thought he might be crying, but then he looked at me.

"Okay," he said. "Sit down."

I sat down. He closed the lid on his laptop and curled his legs cross-legged, winced from knee pain, then uncrossed them.

"Jasmine gave me the pictures. I was an idiot and I didn't tell your mother because that was her best friend, right? And what best friend would, you know—do that? And then your mom found the pictures."

I squinted at him. "You saved them?"

"I told you I was an idiot about it," he said. "It's not like I looked at them or anything. I stuck them in the back of my studio and under a hundred other pictures I kept there. Painters, we…collect pictures and stuff so we can refer to them. Your mom was digging through the pile one day and—well, yeah. That's when things went bad."

He looked sick.

"You mean for her, or for you?"

"For all of us," he said. "Jasmine said she'd stay on the commune and never come here again as long as Darla allowed her to stay on the land. She apologized a lot for the pictures, but your mom wouldn't accept the apologies. Not from me, either."

"So this *is* what caused it?"

"No. Of course not." It sounded like that was probably the three millionth time he'd said it.

"We've never talked about it, you know?" I said.

He nodded vaguely.

"I've always wanted to know…uh." I stopped there. "I

mean, why didn't we leave or make her leave or whatever? Wasn't there a better solution?"

"We didn't know it was coming," he said. "Nobody knew it was coming."

"I don't mean *that*," I said. *That (n.): A better word for suicide.* "I mean before that. I mean, couldn't you just tell Jasmine to go away and show Mom that the pictures were just a—uh—mistake?"

"It was more complicated than that."

"Oh."

"Stuff like that lingers," he said. "And then when Darla died, I could have kicked Jasmine out myself but I didn't because you and Ellie were tight as kids, and how could I take away your only friend at the same time you lost your mom?"

"Shit." I said that because he said *only friend*. I said it because that fact made two secrets into a bigger, more awful secret.

"Yeah."

"That must be hard," I said. "Not talking to her all these years."

"Not talking to Jasmine is easy. Since Darla died, she acts like I'm dead, too," he said. "And where the fuck are those pictures that you saw? I don't want them in the house. I don't want you thinking about this shit."

"Language, Dad."

"Seriously."

"I'm glad you told me this," I said. I looked at him and he smiled at me through a pained face. Transmission from Dad:

One of his ancestors once killed a giant stag by jumping on its back and garroting it with a young tree limb. Still no future for me. No grandchildren fighting or dying in CWII. Just *Megaloceros giganteus.* Just a vision of someone ripping meat from the bone of an enormous drumstick.

My train still felt on track. It felt like its brakes worked. It felt like I could stop it anytime. But I was starting to realize that *Why People Take Pictures* was a turning point. I had never had control of my train. I wasn't sure who, exactly, had control of it. It was different from day to day. Markus Glenn had control the day he asked me to touch his tipi. Ellie had control the days when we were kids and she changed the rules and then, as teenagers, she made me drink the dust of a mummified bat. Dad had control by relinquishing control. I walked through the freight cars and the passenger cars. I walked toward the engine. I wanted to see who was driving. But deep down, I knew who was driving.

Glory O'Brien's History of the Future

The Family Protection Act will spread like lice on a hippie commune. Nine states will draw up similar laws and move them through their legislative branches. They will unofficially secede from the rest of the country, who will think they are bonkers. They will call themselves New America.

There will be a massive rise in welfare applications for single women, single mothers and their children. A massive rise in homeless women and children. A massive rise in random assaults, both violent and sexual, against women and even young girls.

A government official will be quoted as saying, "We're taking our country back!" (From whom? From women and children? Did they take over when none of us were looking? I can't see that in these transmissions, but I doubt it.) Another government official will be quoted as saying, "We gave women two hundred years to reinvent themselves. I think that's long enough."

Women in the media will compare the entire movement to the days of cavemen. Some of them will be confused about what to do or say because they will have unknowingly supported the movement up to the point when they are shown to the studio's door.

And then one state will make a bold move and pass the Fathers Count Law by refusing welfare assistance to any single mother or her children.

I haven't seen what happens after this yet, but it looks like a lot of people starve and a lot of people leave their homes and look for a life somewhere else.

One thing I did see was the collapse of most basic services. Women work in a lot of places. I don't think any of those lawmakers who passed the laws ever thought about what would really happen when they opened the loophole.

Or maybe they did and they just didn't care.

What if we're stuck like this?

Fifty thousand dollars couldn't take me back to an hour before, when I didn't know anything about Jasmine Blue's attempts to steal my father from my mother, and ultimately, me.

Fifty thousand dollars couldn't buy back my father's will to paint. Couldn't buy him a time machine where he could burn those pictures and tell Jasmine Blue to leave him alone before Mom found out.

It couldn't buy Ellie a new life, away from Rick, who was now bugging her about breaking up with him. She said he was passing rumors around the commune.

And it couldn't take me back to Saturday night and stop Ellie and me from drinking the bat.

"What if it never goes away?" she'd asked on the way home from graduation. "What if we're stuck like this forever?"

"Shit," I said.

"Yeah," she said. A minute passed. "But seriously. What if we're stuck like this?"

Her question meant more to me than she'd meant it to. *What if we're stuck like this?* That was the question I'd been asking about Ellie and me for a long time.

I approached the commune's back field, where Jasmine's flock had laid out a bunch of tables with snacks and drinks. I looked for Ellie but she wasn't there yet. At this point, the sky was still pretty bright at the early stages of dusk, and the only planet showing was Jupiter. I stood and listened to the birds in their nests and getting ready to sleep. It was a sound I'd heard a hundred times before, but I'd never really noticed it or something. It was peaceful. It made me feel more comfortable with all my secrets, and now, Dad's secrets.

There was no one around. Maybe they were finishing their dinners. Maybe rolling out their drums from wherever they stored them. Maybe taking naked pictures of themselves to send to other people's husbands—pictures like thin, lightweight atomic bombs that could disintegrate a family in a nanosecond.

Kapow.

"Hey!" Ellie came up from behind me.

"Hey," I said. I told her to stop and listen. "Isn't it weird that birds make completely different noises when they're bedding down to sleep at night than they do in the morning?"

She said, "Duh."

I said, "No, seriously."

She answered, "You need something to eat."

Then we went to the table and loaded up our plates with commune food. I chose two types of paleo crackers made out of what tasted like nuts and berries and pretended to like the almond butter and celery but I hated it, so Ellie took it from me without a word and finished it. It was the friendliest thing she'd done in weeks.

We walked toward a blanket that Ellie had already laid out for us. I admit I was concerned about lice. I sat down anyway.

"Sorry about today," she said. "I was so freaked out. This is so…"

"Messed up," I said.

"Totally," Ellie said. "When I got home I saw Rick. And he's still swearing he didn't give me those…things."

"Huh."

"He said I probably caught it off a toilet seat or something. Like that's even possible."

"It's possible," I said, annoyed that we were still talking about lice. Annoyed that we weren't talking about the history of the future of *everything*.

"Not probable," she said.

"No."

"I saw naked people again. I can't see your war or whatever. None of my naked people are toting guns, anyway."

"Heh." I couldn't help it. The idea of Ellie seeing naked people after seeing those pictures of Jasmine Blue was funny. And every time I looked at Ellie, I saw Jasmine. I was so mad at her again, even though it wasn't her in the pictures.

"I saw my mom has these two great-grandsons. That was cool."

"You saw the grandsons?" I asked.

"Great-grandsons," she said. "So they must be my grandsons, right? Only child and all that."

"Yeah," I said. "That's cool. I can't—uh—I don't see any grandkids in my future, anyway."

This was the closest I'd ever come to telling her my secret. But she wasn't listening.

"So...Rick. I don't know what I'm going to do," she said.

"What is there to do?"

"He lives here."

"And?"

"And I still like him."

I looked at her sideways. "Seriously?"

"I'm...used to him," she said. "That's probably more accurate."

We sat and watched the commune people milling around. I thought about what it must be like to be so free. No jobs. No responsibilities. No rent.

"So, did you get any sweet graduation presents?"

"Just a check from my dad, you know? No party or anything. I mean, why party when there's a party right next door, right?"

More silence. More watching the commune people interact with each other. Even Ellie's dad was out at the food table, loading up a plate.

"Did you get in trouble for coming to graduation?" I asked.

"Double chores when I got back," she said. "I can tell you this: Chickens pretty much have boring futures. Chop chop." She made the motion with her hand. *Chop chop.* "But they're always naked, so at least that's something."

We laughed.

"Did you see much stuff at graduation? I stayed away from people."

"Oh yeah," I answered. "Crazy stuff. Mostly the war."

"Do you think it's real?"

I nodded.

She said, "I see people living in trees. I saw that. And there was this one thing I didn't really understand, but everywhere was flooded and people used boats. It was the future, though, so the boats were really cool. It was hot, too, and no one could use air-conditioning anymore because there was no more oil."

"You're having hippie visions," I said.

"Yeah. I guess."

"I'm having war visions," I said.

"We're going crazy," she said.

"We're not going crazy," I said. "And what's crazy, anyway?"

"I guess."

"How'd you get the marker off your arms?" I asked.

"Special soap we use for poison ivy," she said. She held her arms out for me to see. "It's still there, though. You just have to look really hard."

I looked hard but couldn't see in the near darkness. But I knew what it said.

Free yourself. Have the courage.

"I need a break from this place," Ellie said. "I want to meet complete strangers and find out what I can see about them."

"Tomorrow we should hit the mall," I said. "It's full of complete strangers."

"I hate the mall," she said. It was a reflex. Jasmine hated the mall, so Ellie had to too, even though I'd hidden her consumerist contraband under my bed through middle school.

"It's not like you're going to buy anything," I said. "Trust me. It's a good spot. A lot of different kinds of people."

Dusk fell into night and the stars came out and we lay on our backs and watched the show. Jasmine Blue organized her drum circle and I was right—I couldn't look at her without picturing those pictures.

Very

"How's Glory?" Jasmine asked as I filled my plate with more crackers and cheese. She always called me by my third-person name instead of talking to me like a normal human. Come to think of it, this might have more to do with the same reason Dad wouldn't call her by her name, either.

"Glory is just fine," I answered. I stared at her. *Jasmine's great-great-grandmother was part of the Underground Railroad. She once helped a family of five move through the night and arrive safely at a nearby station only to see them hanged in the morning.*

"I understand you graduated from high school today," she said.

"Indeed."

"Congratulations."

"Thanks," I answered. I could see it on her lips. I could

see it lingering there, but she knew she wasn't allowed to say it. *Your mother would be so proud.*

"I assume you're heading to college to do something wonderful, right?"

"Taking a year off. Figuring myself out. Doing a lot of printing in Darla's darkroom," I said.

"Oh," she said. Trying not to look surprised, but failing. "Wow. How interesting."

"Very," I said.

Then Jasmine Blue Heffner scratched herself. Right at the top of her pubic bone. You know the place. She scratched and then writhed a little in discomfort as if there were a bunch of obligate parasites having their own little star party right there in her pants.

That little scratch made me look around the commune and wonder what I'd do with it if I took it back. I could do that. It was rightfully mine. A bunch of hippie freaks would be released into the world to find jobs and real lives that had nothing to do with drum circles and paleo crackers.

I looked at Jasmine Blue. Transmission from Jasmine Blue Heffner: *Her great-grandsons will be part of the New American Army. One will be an officer of the K division, and the other will be trapped inside a burning house during a battle and will melt like vegan cheese.*

The history of Jasmine's future ended right there.

It made me sad for Ellie, losing her grandsons like that. It made me mad at Jasmine—for everything.

She said something to me, but I didn't hear it over the

melting-like-vegan-cheese great-grandson, so I didn't answer and just kept Jasmine there long enough to make her really uncomfortable. I wanted her to feel like she was in a microwave oven. I wanted her to rotate on the little glass tray. So I looked down at that area—where the Jupiterians might have been living—and I looked back into her eyes before I walked back to the blanket where Ellie was.

"What did you see when you looked at my mom?" she asked. "Did you see my grandsons?"

"Just some really weird shit about your great-great-great-grandmother being part of the Underground Railroad."

"Sweet," she said.

"Sure," I said.

"Rick is here."

I turned my head to see him. "I wonder if he brought his friends from Jupiter."

We laughed. Ellie made her laugh bigger and more animated.

I looked to see what Jasmine Blue's reaction would be to Rick's arrival, but she didn't even look up. I then looked around from woman to woman and I realized none of them looked at Rick. Not one of them. Hard to believe, considering he was wearing a shirt that showed off his tanned, muscular arms.

I said, "I'm going to go and find out what I can find out."

Transmission from Rick: *Rick's grandfather was sent to the Korean War as an eighteen-year-old fresh out of high school. He joined the navy the minute he could so he could go and kill the*

Communists and defeat evil. Rick's father was educated by nuns. They were not nice nuns. They did things to Rick's father that Rick knew nothing about.

"I heard you graduated from Blue Marsh today," he said.

"Yep. I'm a real smarty-pants now," I said.

"Ellie still pissed at me?"

"Um, probably forever, yeah," I said.

"So how come you can come over and talk to me?"

"Because I'm not Ellie," I said. "And because I wanted to tell you that you should stay away from her."

"And?"

I stared at him. Transmission from Rick the dick: *Rick the dick already has two children. One of them lives on this commune. They have curly hair and psoriasis.*

I didn't know what to say after that, so I said, "And nothing. Just stay away from her."

I walked away. He said something to my back, but I don't know what he said. I looked around at the little kids. It was hard to spot psoriasis in the dark.

I lay down on the blanket next to Ellie and watched the stars again. There were two shooting stars in a row, and we gasped and said, "Did you see that?"

I don't know what she saw, but I saw everything from the beginning of time to the end of time—all in those meteors.

We form. We shine. We burn. Kapow.

Glory O'Brien's History of the Future

The Fathers Count Law will be lauded by lawmakers who feel that America has become a welfare state for women who weren't smart enough to use birth control, even though the same lawmakers are on record as being against birth control.

Seems the New America will be run by moronic dipshits. Fantastic.

The Fathers Count Law will also call for the end of child support as we know it—no father who no longer lives with his wife and children will be required to pay for their upkeep. "If those mothers didn't see that fathers count before they left those men, then why should we give them money?"

Chalk up more points for the moronic dipshit team who obviously didn't pay any attention to who-usually-walks-out statistics.

In the small print, the Fathers Count Law will allow a husband to abandon his wife if he feels the wife isn't meeting his personal or domestic needs. But if a woman leaves her husband under any circumstances, she will be breaking the Fathers Count Law.

The key for women will be: If you leave, don't get caught.

So smart

I watched Ellie look from drummer to drummer in the drum circle. Her eyes grew wide sometimes, as if she was seeing the same carnage I was seeing. Or maybe she was seeing other stuff. Rick's DNA trail. Her mother's commune trail. Maybe she would eventually find out that her whole world belonged to me.

Rick stayed by the drum circle. Seeing him reminded me to look around for a little kid with curly hair and bad skin. There were two kids playing over by the campfire. I didn't care enough to go and look at them. So I went to find Mr. Heffner, Ellie's dad. I figured he'd have something interesting to tell me if I looked at him long enough.

Transmission from Ed Heffner: *His father was bald and impotent. His grandfather had been bald and impotent. Ed couldn't help being bald, but he refused to be impotent. And so, he sneaked pills into the commune that helped him not be impotent. His father's last words to him were "Are you ever going to get a job and grow up?" He didn't really like his dad that much. He didn't really like Jasmine all that much. He loved Ellie more than anything.*

"Congratulations," he said to me.

"Thanks."

"Graduation is a big deal," he said. "I didn't think we'd see you here tonight."

"Senior week at the shore isn't really my thing." I'd been invited. I never RSVP'd. "I hope Ellie graduates soon," I said. "It was sad not to have her with me today, seeing we started school together and all."

"I hope she graduates soon, too."

I looked at him. What did I have to lose? "Well, Jasmine rules all, right? What can you do about it?"

He frowned.

I said, "I mean, I couldn't live across the road all this time and not notice that, right?"

"Don't believe everything your dad tells you," he said.

"Really? Because he tells me a lot."

Ed Heffner looked more uncomfortable than he already had. "Well," he said. "It's not as simple as you probably think."

We had a standoff. He stared. I stared. He smiled. I smiled. He frowned. I frowned. Then I said something without even knowing I was going to say it.

"What was my mom like?" This question floated between us. It was an inconvenience. "I mean—was she nice? Funny?

Was she depressed?" I didn't know why I was asking Ed Heffner this, but I was.

"Your mom was funny as hell. So smart," he said. "So smart."

"Huh," I said.

And then silence again—nothing to say.

He looked at his hands. "None of us saw it coming. If we had, I think we would have helped. She'd started working in that mall. She wasn't around much after that. We—uh—were closed-minded about the fact that she got a job."

"She had a job?"

Ed looked uncomfortable again. "Maybe you should ask your dad."

"Sure," I said.

"Things come between friends sometimes," he said.

"They sure do," I said, looking over at Ellie. "I know what things came between Jasmine and my mom."

"Yeah. Jasmine really thought the job was against the whole point of why we moved out here."

"It wasn't the job," I said.

He looked at me. Transmission from Ed Heffner: *His daughter, Ellie, will marry young and he won't be happy about it.*

"Well, what was it, then?" he asked.

"Maybe you should ask Jasmine," I said. "I'm pretty sure she knows."

"Well," he said. "She was a good woman, your mom. You should know that. She left us too soon."

"Thanks," I said. "You're the only person who's ever really

talked to me about her like this." I felt tears forming and my throat closing up around them.

He turned to leave and reached his hand toward my shoulder and squeezed. "Talk to your dad. He can tell you."

"I will," I said, turning from him, too.

Then Ed Heffner walked to his house, opened the door and went in and didn't come out again for the rest of the night. Something about what he said made me want to go back to the darkroom, haunted or not haunted. Why was I afraid of my own mother?

I found Ellie talking to a group of younger kids and got her attention. "I'm going to head home. Long day," I said.

"You'll miss the cake at midnight!"

"I know. It's cool. I'm tired."

"See you tomorrow?" she said. Then she whispered, "Mall?"

I gave her the thumbs-up and walked away from the commune.

————

I went straight into the darkroom and grabbed *Why People Take Pictures* and I opened it to Bill's picture and I stared at it. Then I flipped through it and I found a self-portrait of Darla. It was a Polaroid—cyan highlights, a warm skin tone underneath, shiny and flat—making Darla two-dimensional and ethereal. She looked into the camera in a way that wasn't all there. She stared out at me as if to give me a clue. *I wasn't all there. It wasn't any one thing. It was everything. Because I wasn't all there.*

This was a guess. I wasn't getting transmissions from pictures the way I could get them from living people. But my gut told me I was probably right. *She wasn't all there.* I didn't know if this meant I was off the hook or not. Was I immune to *not all there* or was it coming, out of the blue, like it did for her?

I looked at myself in the reflective black surface of the splashback behind the sink. I looked back at Bill, the man with no head. I flipped to the picture of Darla.

Transmission from Dead Darla: N/A

Transmission from Bill: N/A

Transmission from me: N/A

Looking at Bill freaked me out. There were weirdos who looked at pictures like that on the Internet. I didn't want to be like them. It seemed disrespectful. Maybe Bill had a family. He had to have had a family. Everyone has to come from somewhere, right?

I closed *Why People Take Pictures* and opened one of Darla's other sketchbooks. None of the others had titles. Just numbers. I opened #3 of five.

The first picture was a picture of me. I was a tiny baby. I'd never seen it before and it made me inhale quickly and exhale slowly. It made me afraid to turn the page, but I turned the page anyway.

The next ten pages were pictures of tiny-baby me, too. A few of me with Dad, who looked so young and, frankly, scuzzy. There was one of me asleep on Darla's chest. She had her eyes closed and was smiling. I stared at the picture for a while, but couldn't figure out what I felt. It was a mix.

On the last page of the series, Darla wrote a poem.

I might buy a glistening crystal ball
and lay it down before you.
Roll it between us, and teach you
that the future is round.

And upon shattering it, show you
it is as vast as the shards that
surround us, as sharp as teeth
in living traps.

I will startle you with warnings,
scold you with expectations,
and not confine you to my limits,
but our limits.

Cells made of cells made of cells,
we are a chain of fierce knitting,
a patchwork of relation that
does not fray.

I shall buy a pouch made of leather
and pass it on to you, delicately,
filled with my dust.
Then I will tell you a story.

Underneath the poem, she signed her name. Darla O'Brien. I read the poem about five times. I liked it, but it was morbid or something. Plus, if she thought she'd done anything delicately, she was wrong.

After the poem, there were pictures I already knew—a series of rocks—the same rocks that were upstairs on the living room wall that bored me. Her fascination with rocks was weird. She filled at least forty pages of book #3 with small prints and sketches of them with one repeating question.

What makes a rock a rock?

I took #3 to my room and looked through it as I lay in bed. There were a few pages of chemistry information, but mostly it was more pictures of me and Dad (*Roy After a Day in the Garden* was my favorite) and then more rocks. The rocks made me tired. I fell asleep with one question on my mind.

What makes a rock a rock?

How stuck I felt

I woke just before dawn. I ignored the lying mourning dove.

Before I went downstairs, I looked at my fifty-thousand-dollar check. I could have hopped on a plane to Borneo that day. I could have bought a flashy car or less knobby knees or something. I could have bought an electric oven so I could learn how to bake brownies and broil flounder.

I had no idea what I would do with the money, though, so I sat down and wrote a new entry in *The History of the Future*.

I pieced together everything I saw. I drew a timeline. But I didn't write about what I was thinking. I didn't write about how I wanted to take the commune back from Jasmine Blue because I didn't think she deserved it. I didn't write about Ellie and how stuck I felt.

This book was supposed to serve as a record of how I went crazy. In case…you know. *What makes a rock a rock?* So I wrote all the visions down, and the details about the laws, the armies, the exiles. I didn't write about how I couldn't see my future when I looked at my father. Just a past. I tried to ignore that, even though the longer I ignored it, the more I noticed it.

When I was done, I went down to the darkroom and returned Darla's sketchbook #3 to the shelf and pried *Why People Take Pictures* from behind the cabinet. I opened it to where I'd left it the night before.

> *Bill is following me. He still doesn't have a head.*
>
> *He is telling me something important. He is telling me that there are three of me. I am me. No one special. I am Roy's wife. I am Gloria's mother.*
>
> *It is like juggling.*
>
> *Sometimes I want to drop all the balls and rest my arms. Sometimes I want to stay in this darkroom and sleep until I know which one of me I really am.*
>
> *I have no idea what I'm doing.*
>
> *I have no idea what I'm doing.*

Underneath this was a sketch. It was hard to make out what the sketch was, but when I squinted at it long enough, I saw it. It was a sketch Darla made of herself, but with Bill's head. Or, more accurately, with no head. When the image firmed up and I saw what it was, I turned away. I closed the book.

I opened my sketchbook and I replied to her, minus the morbid sketch. *I have no idea what I'm doing either. I am not juggling anything and I am juggling everything. I can see the whole world's future, but I can't see my own. I can see the whole world's past, but I can't see yours.*

And then I cried—maybe the first real cry I'd had since I was a child. There were so many tears, I was caught off guard. How could there be that many tears stored inside one person?

I remembered crying when I was at school—the times when kids or teachers asked me about my mother. They didn't know any better. They were just normal people with normal lives. *Can we call your mom to pick you up? Can your mom make us something for the end-of-the-year class party? How come your mom doesn't volunteer like my mom does? Does she travel a lot?*

It's hard to understand. I knew that. I was surrounded by people who never had to think about morbid things like I lived with every single day. They never seemed to know how lucky they were.

I cried about the darkroom. I wished I had someone— anyone—to hand me a tissue or find something smart to say. And yet, I'd made sure there was no one. This made me cry harder.

I heard Ed Heffner in my head. I heard him tell me how smart Darla was.

I wanted to believe it so much.

But if she was so smart, then why didn't she see? Why didn't she see what she was doing? Why didn't she understand that one day, I'd be in tenth grade, trying to make friends with the new girl in my class, who would say, "You're so lucky you don't have a mother, Glory. Mine is such a bitch."

Why didn't she understand that once she was gone, Jasmine Blue Heffner would be the only female role model on our road?

Why didn't she understand how lonely Dad would be without her?

I looked back at Bill and I knew the truth. Suicide isn't something people do to hurt other people. It's something people do to release themselves from pain.

My crying lasted an impossible amount of time. It went on forever.

———

Once forever passed, I found a roll of paper towels and cleaned myself up. I didn't want Dad to see I was upset.

The story of my life. I'm not sure why. Maybe it was because I knew he had that many tears stored up, too. If we both started, maybe we wouldn't ever stop.

I noticed my shirt was wet from crying, so I went upstairs to change and I saw the check again. I thought driving to the bank would be a good thing to do. Clear my mind. Maybe even figure out what to do with fifty thousand dollars. So I drove to the bank.

The bank manager was called over because of the amount. Apparently, fifty large makes bank managers anxious. They all fluttered around behind the bulletproof window like chickens locked in a small pen with a hungry rat. Eventually, the steel drawer extended with my receipt and the teller asked me if I needed anything else.

What else could I need?

When I was done at the bank, I drove around. I drove around the neighborhoods. I drove around the old community swimming pool that's overgrown and never open anymore. I drove to the high school and around the empty back parking lot. And then I found the perfect thing to photograph—the empty graduation platform. No one had broken it down yet. It was just 350 empty chairs and an empty stage with empty steps and empty bleachers and an empty sky and an empty podium.

Day one, post–graduation from high school: This was the first day of the rest of my life. And it was empty, just like everything else. Zone 10 was in the shiny reflection off the white stage awning. Zone 0 was in the shadows beneath the makeshift handicapped ramp and the chairs.

I metered the scene and took a roll of pictures. I titled them in my head. *Empty Chairs. Empty Stage. Nobody's Talking at the Podium.* When I was done, I walked to the away bleachers where Ellie had been the day before. I looked for her graffiti.

Free yourself. Have the courage. WHO IS THE PETRIFIED BAT? That was in all caps. *WHO IS THE PETRIFIED BAT?* I sat on the dewy-damp concrete and asked myself. *Who is the petrified bat?* Then I pulled a black Sharpie marker from my purse and answered. I wrote: *I Am the Petrified Bat.* I wrote it ten times, in ten different ways. I took pictures of each one and went home.

When I looked at my negatives once I'd developed them and hung them to dry, I saw each angle as a point of view.

That was what a picture was, wasn't it? A point of view? If you took a picture of a glass from above, it would look mostly empty. If you took it from below, it would look half full. A clichéd example, but you understand. Everything we see is based on where we're standing when we see it.

Maybe my mother went crazy. Maybe she didn't. Maybe she was really being followed by Bill, the man with no head. Maybe Bill existed. Maybe Bill didn't exist. Maybe he existed just for her, as a message from somewhere else. From *over there*. Or from *down there*. Or from *up there*. Maybe it all depended on your point of view.

Glory O'Brien's History of the Future

Nedrick the Sanctimonious will come from an unconventional place. He will not be born to wealthy parents. He will not be a politician. He will not even go to college. He will be an electrician—and not a very good one. His friends will call him Ned.

It will take a year for the Second Civil War to start, but Nedrick will have every intention of war as he begins his K-Duty Club. He will gather his friends after closing time at their local bar and they will travel forty-five miles to cross the border into Old America. They will steal girls.

Some nights they will steal as many as ten. Some nights they may only find one or two. They won't discriminate. They will steal a white girl as fast as they'll steal a black girl, though they will prefer young teenagers because they will be the easiest to sell. I'm not sure who they sell them to. I can only see that they drive home with wads of cash in their pockets.

Nedrick the Sanctimonious will love to talk about the Family Protection Act and the Fathers Count Law. He himself will be free of a ten-year-old forty-five-thousand-dollar child support bill thanks to the latter. He will be a natural speaker with an ego so large, he will say aloud that he is the smartest man in the world. He will name himself Nedrick the Sanctimonious.

He will not figure out that he is the biggest moronic dipshit of all.

Ellie didn't give a shit about chlorofluorocarbons

"Are we still going to the mall or what?" Ellie asked.

Dad had let her in and into the basement, but the minute I'd heard the basement door open, I hid *Why People Take Pictures* and left the darkroom because I didn't want her in there. I didn't want her near any of it. My pictures. Darla's pictures. Pictures of Jasmine Blue, her naked mother. I walked her up and into the living room.

I saw Ellie looking at Dad and I could see she was seeing his infinity and I wondered if she saw any future. I wanted him to have a future. I wanted *me* to have a future. I hoped she would be honest with me even though I hadn't been honest with her. I wanted to know if my grandsons would be part of the machine. I wanted to know if my granddaughters would be stolen. I wanted to know everything... if there was anything. I was so tired of empty.

We got into the car.

"What did you see when you looked at my dad?" I asked.

She shrugged. "Something about his feet. How he has his mother's feet."

I wanted to ask her about his future. Maybe grandkids. Maybe great-grandkids. I didn't say anything, though, and just drove toward the mall.

"Can we stop at a coffee place?" Ellie asked me.

I pulled into a Dunkin' Donuts and lined up in the drive-thru. She ordered something fancy. I ordered a bottle of water.

"So, this war," she said as we waited. "It's going to affect our grandkids. And it's going to be what? I can't get it. Girls are stolen? For what?"

"I think the usual girls-in-war stuff. I've seen them being sold."

"Like prostitution?" she asked. "Doesn't seem logical."

We pulled to the window and I paid because I knew Ellie didn't have money. She slurped her coffee drink as we drove around the winding road to the mall.

"I mean, if they sell all the girls, then who's left to make new people?" she asked.

"Good point," I said. "They call it K-Duty. They don't always steal girls. Some just hunt and kill people. They call it the machine."

"That's creepy," she said.

"Yeah," I said. "The whole idea of another civil war is creepy if you ask me."

"I don't get it," she said. "How can we divide over anything anymore? It's not like we still have slavery, right?"

"I don't know," I said. "I think it has something to do with politics."

I don't know why I didn't tell Ellie about some of the things I knew. I saved the facts for the book because sometimes, certain people don't want to hear stuff like that. Ellie didn't believe women had any farther to go, right? So if I'd told her about the Fathers Count Law or any of that, she probably would have thought I was making it up out of my own agenda.

We sat in a parking space for a minute with the AC cranked because Ellie didn't give a shit about chlorofluorocarbons—not when she was away from Jasmine Blue, anyway. A college-aged kid pulled into the space next to us. We both looked at him and he looked back at us.

Transmission from the college kid in the mall parking lot: *His distant descendant will be a leading Godcaster in the twenty-seventh century. His broadcasts will be seen by ten billion people a day. His charity will collect over fifty trillion dollars in the name of Christianity. He will go to jail because he will steal several billion dollars of this money in order to pay for his addiction to sports cars. He will be euthanized at the start of the Third Intergalactic War because he will be over fifty years of age. His four hundred sports cars will be discovered in an enormous barn on Earth in Western Kentucky.*

The twenty-seventh century. Wow. And still . . . more war.

"What did you see?" I asked Ellie.

"His grandfather insisted on using the same fork and napkin ring at every meal. He'd travel with the fork and napkin ring. They didn't even match. But he insisted, so until he died, he ate with the same fork and rolled his napkin in the same ring."

"Wow."

"You?"

I told her what I'd seen about the kid's crazy descendant in the twenty-seventh century.

She said, "I wonder why we get such different versions."

"Dunno," I answered, knowing it was just like earlier in the darkroom. It all depended on where we were standing, right?

We got out of the car and stepped into a humid Pennsylvania day. As we walked through the parking lot she asked, "What were you doing in your basement today?"

"Just some work in the darkroom."

"Huh. I didn't know you were into that."

"I have a summer project I want to do," I said. "Nothing formal. I just always wanted to get into printing, you know?"

"That's cool," she said. "I bet that's cool for your dad, right?"

I shrugged. "He seems weird about it," I said. "I look like her, you know?"

She nodded as we walked through the double doors into the mall. "You do. I've seen pictures."

Oh, Ellie. And you look like your mom, too.

As we walked to the food court, where Ellie vowed to eat the most processed and disgusting food she could find, which wouldn't be hard, she said, "Do you really think Rick gave me those... the Jupiterians?"

I said, at the same time, "Did you see anything in my dad's future when you looked at him before we left?"

We looked at each other and laughed. I don't know why I was laughing. I was stuck in a mall with Ellie, who was so self-centered that she only ever wanted to talk about her own pubic lice.

I answered her question. "Yes."

She answered my question. "No."

Then we found a booth in the food court and made it our home base. It was central to the eating area and we would see plenty of people during lunch hour, which was coming any minute. Ellie went to buy a variety of disgusting microwaved Mexican food at Señor Burrito and I was tortured by lunch foods and wasn't hungry. I locked eyes with a woman who looked about forty. She had several shopping bags next to her on the empty chairs at her table.

Transmission from shopping lady: *Her granddaughter will be part of a rebel group that will blow up the busiest train station in New America. She will go to jail for this, and after jail she will be sent to Camp #32.*

I wanted to pretend that I was as crazy as Darla when I saw things like that. I would rather have stuck my head in an oven and denied my family any future at all if that was what it was going to look like.

"You look like you saw a ghost," Ellie said to me, returning with her tray of gross food and a tray of plain nachos for me.

I did see a ghost. I saw a ghost of everything that is good in the world dying.

"They steal them to make them breeders," I said. "In breeder camps."

Ellie took a too-hot bite of her cheese enchilada and fanned her mouth. Then she said, "Shit."

Ferret Company will sniff out exiles

Just a Tuesday lunch hour at the mall. Just two country girls hanging out eating nachos in flip-flops and shorts. The older women had tans already. Some of them had babies in strollers. Some of the baby-stroller women were young. As young as us, maybe. Some had tattooed boyfriends in baseball caps. Some had boyfriends in business suits. They all seemed to scorn each other.

It was one big competition, this food court.

People drew lines.

The food court was just like everything else now: Divisive. Self-righteous. Hopeless. I could totally see why a second civil war was on its way...if it wasn't just in my bat-ingesting head.

Transmission from the tattooed baby-daddy in the baseball cap: *His grandfather escaped a gunfight in Vietnam that killed twenty-one in his platoon. He came home to find that his*

wife had had a kid with someone else, so he hitchhiked all the way
to Crescent City, California, where he discovered giant redwood
trees and decided they were the most beautiful creatures on the
planet. Even more beautiful than his wife, who'd had a baby
with someone else while he was getting shot at in Vietnam. So he
stayed there. He wrote a letter home to his wife only once. It said,
"Thank you."

"See that girl over there?" Ellie said to me. "Her ancestors were Lenape Indians. They used to carve arrowheads and hunt, like, ten miles from here. Her great-great-great-grandmother was a talented weaver and died from tuberculosis."

I looked around. The food court was filling up. It was a mix of mall employees, shoppers, mall rats and the old guys who sit on the benches all day and people-watch. I got transmissions from some of them, but nothing about the war.

Then the old guy in the wheelchair showed up.

Transmission from a wheelchair-bound old guy with a big smile and a USS *Pledge* baseball cap: *His father was a great talker and he never got a word in edgeways. So he took the role of the quiet kid. When his father died, he was finally able to hold real conversations and be funny. He was sixty-one when that happened. He regrets it taking that long. Also, his great-great-grandson will somehow hurt my family during the Second Civil War. Something involving fire and a tunnel.*

The way he looked at me, it was like he could see infinity, too. Or maybe I was staring at him. Anyway, his great-great-grandson would hurt the O'Briens. And there is a tunnel.

"Are you seeing tunnels anywhere?" I asked Ellie.

"Tunnels?" she asked, still looking at the kid she was reading. "No tunnels. I see, like, hospitals or something. Not like I've ever been to a hospital."

She meant the camps. They looked like hospitals. "No tunnels, though?"

"Nope."

Something told me I needed to know more about the tunnels, so I looked back at the old man in the USS *Pledge* hat. Another transmission: *The tunnels will be filled with smoke and there will be no escape. Before the smoke, the tunnels will facilitate an exodus...an exodus led by the women who live in the trees.*

I blinked. I'd seen visions of women in the trees before. Why would women live in the trees?

More transmission: *His great-great-grandson will own a bright red pickup truck. It will have a bumper sticker on it that says* MY OTHER TOY HAS TITS. *He will wear a uniform that sports the letter* K *in a yellow circle. He will steal girls from over the border even though there are border patrols. Eventually he will be promoted to the head of Ferret Company. Ferret Company will sniff out exiles.*

I was scared of this guy. Not just of the great-great-grandson who wasn't born yet, but of the man in the wheelchair. It was like he was sent to freak me out. Why didn't I see anything mundane? Why not some bizarre journey to his German ancestors in lederhosen? A quick jaunt to life on the USS *Pledge*? A date with a cute girl in one of those 1950s dresses that puffed out at the knees?

Ellie asked, "You okay?"

I spun myself around away from the wheelchair guy. "Yeah."

"No you're not," she said.

"He freaked me out," I said. "That's all."

"All I'm getting is boring crap," she said, and motioned toward the middle-aged manager of the pizza place with the really great calzones. "That guy? His father was a plumber in Newark, New Jersey. He was known for his expertise in unclogging toilets." She rolled her eyes. "I have a fucking superpower and all I get are plumbers and napkin ring stories. Great."

"Let's stop for a minute," I said.

She looked at me. "You sure you're okay? What the hell is he looking at?" she said, looking over my shoulder.

"Is he still looking?"

"Yeah."

"Shit."

"Who is he?" she asked.

"I have no idea. But his great-great-grandson is going to hurt my family and do a lot of bad shit to people."

"No shit," she said. "Maybe we should kill him now."

"It's already done. If we wanted to kill anyone, it would be the son or the grandson."

"Geez, Glory. I wasn't serious."

"I'm getting a calzone," I said, and I got up. Instead of walking away from the wheelchair guy, I walked right up to him and then around him to the Italian place. He spun around and followed me.

"Do I know you?" he asked.

"No," I said. "I don't think so."

"You look familiar," he said.

"Huh. Well, maybe I look like someone you know."

"Sorry about that," he said. He put his smile back on. "I must be mistaking you for someone else."

Clearly he was just some old guy who couldn't see all that well.

As I stood in line for my calzone, it became clear that this man's great-great-grandson couldn't do anything to my family if there wasn't a future beyond Glory O'Brien—if Glory O'Brien didn't live long enough to have a kid or something.

This felt freeing—as if I could shake off Darla and Bill and all the other fates that had been haunting me. I could have a future. Maybe a kid…or two. Maybe a career or a hobby or something that wasn't as hollow and empty as day one postgraduation.

I smiled. But then I was horrified. What kind of a cruel joke is it to know that any family I create will only be stuck in this hell? A hell where girls are stolen and bred? Where boys are made to fight wars they don't want to fight?

I looked around the food court. I saw the baby-daddies. I saw the women in fake tans and formal hairdos. I saw a little girl wearing makeup eating lunch with her mom. I saw the third button on Ellie's shirt undone, exposing just enough.

I grabbed my calzone, threw a ten-dollar bill at the owner and escaped.

You can tell by the hair

"I don't get why we had to leave right then," Ellie said. "It's not like anything happened."

"I had a panic attack. Or whatever they are," I said, driving down 422. "I couldn't breathe."

"You can get pills for those," she said.

"What's that mean?"

"It means you could have just walked around with me and we could have stayed. It's my only day away, you know? I wanted it to last longer than a lousy hour."

I called conversations like this *Everything's About Ellie*. It was a TV show in my head and there was a laugh track. *It's my only day away, you know?* [Insert laugh track laughter.] *I wanted it to last longer than a lousy hour.* [Insert laugh track laughter.] If Ellie Heffner had panic attacks, the world would stop for her. But me? I'd just have to suck it up because it was her *only day away*.

She'd tried, in the food court, to get me to change my mind with manipulative huffs and noises and faces but I just gathered my stuff and headed down the escalator, which only made the whole thing worse. By the time I got to the bottom, I not only couldn't breathe, but I was also dizzy and felt like I had to vomit.

Then the elevator door opened to my right and the USS *Pledge* guy in the wheelchair came out and the panic was vast.

Just the thought of a future—mixed with the thought of my someday procreating—nearly knocked me out. I knew I couldn't say this to Ellie. Ellie would think I was either being a prude or dumb or overreacting to something that seems normal to most people.

To me, living long enough to have a kid was never guaranteed.

To me, bringing a kid into a world that was about to collapse was a mistake.

Was this what Darla felt? That bringing a kid into the world she saw—the world in *Why People Take Pictures*—was a mistake?

All of these things descended when he wheeled out of the elevator. And so I took off through the main doors. And then I ended up on 422 driving us home.

Oh well.

"Can we go somewhere else now that you're calmed down?" Ellie asked.

I pulled into the McDonald's parking lot. I said, "I'm not calmed down. Panic attacks are serious. It's not a matter of just *calming down*."

"Sorry."

I sighed. "We can go somewhere else if you want. I just need some time away from people."

"Even me?" she asked.

"Even you." Things were breaking in my head. I needed time away from people. I needed time away from everything.

"Well, then drop me back at the mall and go driving or something."

[Insert laugh track laughter.]

I don't know why I got so angry with her so quickly. Actually, I don't think it was all that quickly. I think it started a long time ago and I was just holding it in. And now I felt it rise in me and rush out of my mouth.

I said, "Rick has two kids."

She said, "What the hell are you talking about?"

I said, "Just look around over there."

"Over where?"

"On your mother's commune," I said. "They live there. Or one of them does, anyway."

She looked at me as if I'd just slapped her and I did just slap her. It's a very dangerous thing, knowledge. The bat was a very dangerous companion.

"Rick is only nineteen," she said. "You're so full of shit."

I didn't say anything.

"How do you know this? You saw it? In who?"

"In Rick. Last night. At the party."

I could feel her glaring at me, but she didn't say anything.

"I think he's slept with other women there, you know," I

said. I didn't say *maybe including your mother* but I didn't have to. It would sink in.

"That's bullshit."

"You saw him with Rachel's mom," I said.

She steamed. I saw it pouring out of her. Hot steam. "This shit isn't real, Glory. Stop believing it as if it's real," she said. There was silence in the car as I drove back through the mall parking lot. Then Ellie said, "You're probably just jealous, anyway."

"Jealous of what?"

"I had sex first."

"That makes no sense."

"You're pissed because I didn't tell you," she said. "But I didn't tell you because I knew you weren't mature enough to handle it."

"You have no idea how mature I am."

"I know you never had a boyfriend. I know that. So how would you know anything about anything?"

"I don't need a boyfriend to know things, Ellie."

"You're trying to get Rick and me to break up because you're jealous."

I stopped the car outside the mall entrance. "Just go," I said.

"Admit it."

I looked at her.

"Admit that you're just jealous."

"I'm not jealous. I'm not anything. I was just telling you what I saw. Rick has two kids. That's all I know. It could be bullshit. This could all be bullshit, okay? We're going crazy, right? We drank a fucking bat, all right? What the hell do I know? I was just telling you what I saw."

She was halfway out of the car when I said this and she turned around to say something, but I hit the accelerator a little so she'd just shut the door and get out.

As I drove to the mall exit I started to cry again. This was not a good day for me and crying. I felt like such an idiot for letting Ellie into my life this week. It was supposed to be my freedom week.

I drove around for a while to get my tears back into my body where they belonged. I eventually got to where I wanted to be—the library main branch. I went to the research librarian and I asked her to point me toward the war section.

"I'm looking for tunnels," I said. "What wars had tunnels?"

She shrugged. "I'm pretty sure most wars have them."

"What about the Civil War?" I asked.

She searched her computer and then handed me a printout about the tunnels in Vicksburg, Mississippi, during the Civil War. Then she took me to the stacks and found me two other books. One about the Korean War and one about Vietnam, both about tunnels. Then she got me a copy of *The Great Escape* on DVD and sent me to the front desk. After I checked them out, I sat in a quiet corner of the library and read. Tunnels were scary things. Very scary things. They collapsed, they could be infiltrated from both sides and trap people. They could be burned up. As a girl prone to anxiety and mild claustrophobia, tunnels made me feel generally like peeing in my pants. I was hoping my descendants would not inherit my irrational fears.

Two hours later, my panic attack was long gone and I got a message on my cell from the pay phone at the mall from Ellie, who was ready to be picked up and driven to her next destination. [Insert laugh track laughter.] I went to the mall and picked her up and she didn't say anything to me about Rick. She didn't apologize to me about calling me jealous or implying that I was stupid.

She did say, "I'm sorry about telling you to calm down or whatever. I know you can't do anything about it."

"Thanks."

"Want to go out for dinner?"

"Nah. I need to get home. I haven't had any time since graduation and I have shit to do."

"Chinese takeout?" she offered.

"No thanks," I said.

The silence wasn't awkward for me. I didn't squirm through it. I didn't have anything to say.

"I know which kid is his," she finally said. "Rick's, I mean." She looked out the window. "You can tell by the hair."

"Yeah," I said.

"And the kid is almost two," she said. "Which means he's been doing this for a while."

"Yeah."

"The day I leave that place will be the best day of my life," she said.

"Sorry about blurting it out, but I thought you should know," I said. "Probably not the best way to tell you."

"Sorry I said all those things," she said. "It hasn't been a great week."

"No shit."

Awkward silence.

"Will you still talk to me after this?" [Insert laugh track laughter.]

"I don't know."

"We can't go through this bat stuff without having each other," she said.

"I've been through plenty of stuff by myself without your help," I said.

"What's that supposed to mean?"

"It means exactly what I said."

"What stuff? Did you have a boyfriend that you didn't tell me about?"

I rolled my eyes. "Why does everything with you have to be about a boyfriend? Jesus! You're obsessed," I said. "Look—fine. Go sleep with Rick again. Marry him. I don't care. Just don't ask me to get more crab killer for you, okay?"

"I don't get what you've been through," she said. "I was asking. You don't have to be so bitchy."

"You don't get what I've been through?"

Awkward silence.

She said, "Well, are you going to tell me?"

"Forget it," I said.

"Is it your mom and how she—uh—killed herself?"

"Just forget it," I said.

"I never talked to you about that because I thought you were over it," she said.

I stayed quiet as we drove the final mile home. If I'd opened my mouth, a dragon would have flown out and would have flamed Ellie so badly in my car, she'd have been nothing but a pile of stupid, selfish, boy-obsessed ashes.

Glory O'Brien's History of the Future

The Second Civil War will start with a bomb. It will be a very big bomb. I am beginning to think that whatever happened to me happened so I would know this stuff and do something about it. But what can a seventeen-year-old girl do about anything? I can't even vote.

From what I saw, the explosion, in a state capitol building, will kill seven state senators and many capitol staff. The media will go wild, which will be nice because before the bomb, the media will have already stopped reporting nightly on the disappearance of girls from the border states of New America.

But the bomb will change all of that, because Nedrick the Sancti-monious will get on the airwaves and declare war.

It's not like no one will see this coming. Nine states will have already seceded and become their own bizarre country. Ten states will have already forced women to stop working. But no one will know New America is going to *war*. No one will know New America has an *army*.

Nedrick will say, "You all thought we were stupid hillbillies. Guess you might want to rethink that."

The president will amass the National Guard. It will take a month for him to realize that he will need more than the National Guard.

Am I making sense?

After I dropped Ellie off at the commune, I drove to the nearest Chinese restaurant and got the spiciest food I could order because from the minute Ellie mentioned it, I wanted some. I ordered Dad an egg roll and a large pad Thai, his favorite from that place.

As I drove I tried to block out what Ellie had said, but it was hard.

I thought you were over it.

People are so stupid sometimes.

When I got home, Dad was AWOL, so I sat at the kitchen table by myself and ate my dinner facing the place where the oven used to be. It was a vacuum of not-oven. I stared at it because I knew particles of my mother were still there somehow.

I looked at the vacuum of not-oven and I thought: *I will somehow create a descendant. And that descendant will be trapped in a tunnel near the end of the Second Civil War.*

I was pissed that I hadn't talked to the USS *Pledge* man when I saw my future in him. I had so many questions, and he might have the answers. Maybe more visions of a baby or something. Anything.

I smiled even though I'd never liked babies. The first baby I ever held was my aunt Amy's daughter when she was less than a month old and all Aunt Amy did the whole time was screech about how I had to hold the kid's head up as if her precious God would make a creature so frail that not holding its head up every single second could snap it off like a dry twig.

I stared at the kitchen cabinet that had replaced the oven and wondered what it was like to bake bread or make a pie or roast a chicken or do any of those oven-themed things. Things that didn't taste like radiation. Things that suffered real-oven side effects. Things that got crispy and browned. Things that rose or fell. If I was going to live past eighteen, I wanted those things.

I opened my fortune cookie. *Everything serves to further.*

Huh.

Everything serves to further.

I looked up at the not-oven vacuum. I decided to tell Dad that I planned on using part of my fifty thousand dollars to buy a new oven—electric—so I could learn to be a normal human. It was about time, right? To be normal?

Like anything about life after the bat is normal. Like anything could ever be normal knowing what I know—about now or the future.

I returned to the darkroom after dinner to find my negatives dry and *Why People Take Pictures* behind the cabinet where I'd left it. Where Darla had left it. I wanted to sit there all night and read the whole thing now that I had time.

I opened it to the next page and it was a two-page spread of old-time pornography. Nothing too shocking, mind you. Calendar stuff. Bikini-clad models on the beach, then bikini-clad models on the beach missing their tops. Then formerly-bikini-clad models on the beach showing their tan lines. Under each one, Darla wrote captions.

You.
Are.
All.
Worth.
More.
Than.
This.

On the next page there were two pretty gross pictures of Jasmine Blue Heffner. Her legs were—uh—open. It was—uh—uncomfortable. Not just because I was looking at Jasmine Blue Heffner's privates, but because I knew she'd given these pictures to Dad. And because I knew Darla had found them. And I knew it must have crushed her. I turned the page and found a large picture of a tub of anti-aging cream. Under it, Darla wrote:

You're a pornographer too, you know.

On the next page was a self-portrait. Darla was plain and beautiful. Her eyes looked like she'd seen a ghost. Underneath, it read:

I have wrinkles. I am not tortured by them. I am no one special and so what if I have wrinkles? One day I will be no one special and be dead. Am I making sense?

I stared at that last paragraph for a while and I wished I had Darla and her wrinkles rather than Dead Darla. Live Darla sounded like she would be fun to talk to. Honest. Not scared to say shit that most people are scared to say. Live Darla probably would have great taste in music. She might have had wrinkles, but she would have shown me around that dark-room and made me feel like I belonged there instead of feeling like a burglar.

I doled out three trays and started the print washer. It made a swooshing noise that calmed me as I mixed developer, stop bath and fixer for the trays. I stared at the setup. It was so simple, wasn't it?

No microchips or megabytes or silicone or software. Just chemistry and water. Just silver on paper. Just light and darkness.

I inspected my dry negatives and cut them into strips and put them on the countertop in order. I turned on the amber light and hit the main switch so the room got dark. It was quieter then, inside the room and inside my head. Everything was quieter. I got some glass and risked some of Darla's old 8 x 10 paper and I made three contact sheets of my negatives. *So simple. Light shines on the paper, through the negative, makes a tiny picture.* Then I slipped the paper into the developer and moved the tray back and forth until the image formed. By the time I was finished and the contact sheets were in the dryer, I understood the therapeutic value of Darla's darkroom.

I thought again about what Ellie had said. How could anyone think I would be over it? I thought about the thirteen years I'd lived while no one ever talked about it. I thought about how I always thought people just had a problem with death. I'd read articles. It's true. People totally have a problem with death. But what's worse is the problem they have afterward. They just don't know what to say. They still have normal lives to get on with. They still have ovens.

I wanted to talk to Dad, but I was mad at him. For a list of things it was too late to bring up now.

I wanted to talk to Ellie, but I was mad at her, too.

Why hadn't either of them helped me? Why hadn't they asked? Wasn't it obvious? Was it that hard to connect the dots of Glory O'Brien? Or had I been so good at hiding everything that they'd simply done exactly what I needed them to do... even though I needed them to do something entirely different?

It wasn't Ellie's responsibility to make sure I was okay.

Dad should have at least brought it up once by now.

I turned on the main light and opened some of Darla's regular not-secret, not-hidden-behind-the-print-dryer sketchbooks. They were wonderful. So many obscure images of life. So many smart captions. So many indications that she was once happy. All there. Not crazy. Not ready to go. But then there was this one picture. It was of me and Dad. The caption read: *When I'm with them, I feel trapped inside a latex balloon.*

It's like witnessing an amazing father and his adorable daughter walking down the other side of the street.

I knew that feeling.

I knew what it was like to be in a latex balloon. It was suffocating. Somehow this connection didn't make me cry. It made me understand a little. It made me wonder what I could do to get out of the balloon.

Then, as I turned toward the door, something caught my eye.

The tooth.

She'd hung it from the ceiling over the door, like morbid mistletoe. It shimmered—reflecting back to me, through Darla.

It had a small fortune-sized message attached to it. I stood on the stool and reached out with shaky hands to read it. It said: *Not living your life is just like killing yourself, only it takes longer.*

BOOK THREE

The road to nowhere

The train is yours. You don't have to go anywhere
you don't want to. You don't have to pick up any
passengers or cargo. You can go it alone. Sometimes
there will be tunnels. Sometimes there will be baking
sunlight. It all depends on where you steer.

Shit, Cupcake

Dad looked scared of what I was going to say next. I didn't blame him. I was talking a mile a minute and must have said "Darla" six times. It wasn't fair. But I needed to know.

So I slowed down.

"Why did Darla say she was a pornographer?" I asked.

"Shit, Cupcake. Where are you reading this stuff?"

"I was meant to read it. She wrote it for me. But she didn't tell me details. So you have to tell me."

He sighed and sat down at the kitchen table. "She took a job at that photo lab at the mall because she wanted access to a color processor. The owner worked out a deal with her, you know? She printed what orders were given to her. Some was that kind of stuff, I guess. It wasn't good for her."

It wasn't good for her. Oh well.

"Wilson used to take these calendar shots," he added. "Not like the stuff you see now."

"Ew. Mr. Wilson was a pornographer?"

"Can we stop using that word?"

"Okay," I said. "Mr. Wilson took naked pictures of people? Is that better?"

He looked pained.

"Did he take the ones of Jasmine Blue?"

"How do I know?"

"Oh."

"Don't look at me like that," he said.

"Like what?"

"Like I'm some kind of pervert."

I didn't know what to say to that. For all my crying that day, I was still mad at him for never talking about it. Maybe he thought I was over it too, like Ellie did. Maybe he kept the pictures Jasmine gave him because it was nice to be wanted. Because it is, right? Nice to be wanted?

"What?" he asked.

"You weren't even a little bit flattered that Jasmine wanted you to be—you know."

"No."

"So why'd you keep the pictures?"

"Look," he said. "Your mother and I were soul mates. Monogamous. Not like it's any of your business, but I never slept with anyone in my life except your mother. Not before, not since."

"Huh," I said. And then I felt sad, because it seemed too long for Dad to be without—um—sex. I mean, Darla was dead thirteen years.

But I understood. When someone you love chooses to go that way, a large part of you dies along with them. I don't know how else to explain it. I was four and I understood it. I was now seventeen and I understood it.

They take you with them.

"Sorry," he said. "I didn't want to make you uncomfortable. I just—I don't want you to think the wrong thing about us, either."

"So what's with the tooth?" I asked.

He looked puzzled and then he smiled. "Is that still there? Wow. I forgot all about it."

"Still there."

"Number forty-six," he said, pointing to his jaw where number forty-six usually resides in the human mouth. "She had to get it pulled," he said. He frowned. "She wasn't herself after that."

"Wasn't herself?"

"The job. The tooth. All of it kinda came down on her. She wasn't the same."

"You think that's what did it?" I asked.

"She was depressed. I told her. She kept saying it was just a phase. That she would solve it."

We sat there silently.

"She solved it, all right," I said.

He started to tear up then. This wasn't something he did. So I joined him, considering I'd had plenty of practice that day already.

We cried. Then we hugged. Then we blew our noses and

he made the elephant sound he always makes when he blows his nose and it annoyed me like it does every time. And then we laughed because he knew he'd annoyed me.

"She wouldn't get help. Escaped into her darkroom. And then the shit hit the fan with those damn pictures."

I didn't know what to say. This was the most we'd ever talked about...anything.

"I could have helped her. But she was so mad at me," he said.

"It wasn't your fault," I said.

"You know when I found her, you were in the living room with her shoes?"

"Her shoes?" I didn't remember this.

"You were hugging her shoes. And you'd put all your acorns into one of them and you wouldn't let me have them back."

"God. I don't remember that," I said.

He was crying full force now. I'd never seen him like this. "I relive it every day, you know?"

"I want us to get on with our lives," I said. "I want you to start painting and stop feeling like it's some guilty pleasure. It's not."

He looked at me while he wiped his eyes with the palm of his hand. "All I've wanted to do since the day Darla died was move somewhere else. Take back that land." He pointed toward the commune. "Sell up and get out, you know? California. Or Italy. Or the Virgin Islands. Maine. Vermont. I don't care where. I can't function here." He pointed toward the kitchen to the space where the oven was. "Every day I see her there."

I stared into his bloodshot, tear-filled eyes.

Transmission from Dad: *His father didn't talk to him much after Darla died. He didn't know what to say, so he didn't say anything. On his deathbed, he said, "Sorry about your girl, son." His mother hadn't talked to him in twenty-five years, since she left to be a tree-hugging hippie who traveled with a group called the Skyforce Coalition, who may or may not have believed in the existence of benevolent unicorns. She didn't know I existed. She didn't even know Darla was dead.*

Now *that's* convenient.

Everything serves to further

Dad's crying was big. I asked him if he needed anything and he shook his head no. I wanted to give him space so I told him I'd be back in a little while and I went to the darkroom. I checked on the print dryer, and the contact sheets were dry.

I got the scissors and cut out the little negative-sized pictures and I stuck them into my sketchbook and taped my fortune under it.

Everything serves to further.

I wrote it, too. *Everything serves to further.*

I opened *Why People Take Pictures*. I heard Dad blowing his nose upstairs and wondered if one day I should show him the book. Or if maybe he'd seen it and left it hidden for me to find. Maybe this was all planned. Maybe he wanted me to meet Darla on my own terms. Or maybe he wanted me to meet Jasmine on my own terms. You choose.

Next page was a smaller print of Bill—the man with no head. Above it was this: *I saw Bill again today. He was in the darkroom with me. Still no head.*

Below it was this: *Why did you shoot your head off?*

As I read those words, *Why did you shoot your head off?*, I realized that Darla had been trying to find the answer to the same question I was. I didn't know when her quest started— was it early in life? Had she wondered since she'd heard about it the first time? When do normal people really think about suicide for the first time? Darla was seven when Jim Jones slaughtered his followers in Jonestown and called it mass suicide. Maybe she'd seen it on the news. Maybe it came later, in art school when she learned about Diane Arbus, one of her favorite photographers, who died in 1971—the year Darla was born. Maybe it was Kurt Cobain in '94. Roy and Darla were big fans.

The more I looked at that page—*Why did you shoot your head off?*—and compared it to my page—*Everything serves to further*—the more the two blended together. Maybe I'd found Darla her answer.

Why did he shoot his head off?

Because everything serves to further.

Even if it makes no sense.

Even if it leaves behind a hole so big you can't breathe some days.

My phone rang. It was Ellie. I ignored it and let her leave a voice mail. And then I checked the voice mail because for all my pretending, I was still on the fence about our friendship... even if she was a dipshit.

"Hey, Glore. Can you call me back? I have to talk to you."

I didn't call her back.

But everything serves to further. Even inaction.

Everything serves to further. Even naked pictures that your best friend gives to your husband.

Everything serves to further. Even birthing a baby who will birth another baby who will die in a smoke-filled tunnel sometime in the future.

There's got to be another door

I **went back upstairs** to Dad on the couch. He wasn't crying anymore, and he looked emotionally lighter, if there is a way to look emotionally lighter. "Do you hate Jasmine Blue?" I asked.

He thought about the question for a few seconds. Rubbed his chin. "Yeah. I pretty much do."

"I think I'm starting to hate Ellie, too," I said.

"Let's not use the word *hate*, okay, Cupcake? Your mom would freak out."

I sputter laughter. "Like *she* didn't hate Jasmine after she found those pictures? Yeah right."

"She didn't. She kinda felt sorry for her. Same as she felt sorry for all those other women—you know—in compromising positions."

"And then she committed suicide, Dad."

He looked at me.

"If that's not an act of hate, I don't know what is," I said.

"She hated the world," he said. "She was mad as hell at the world." He looked at his hands then. "I always figured it was her final joke—leaving us on her own terms. Getting the hell out of here. All the politics. All the bullshit. Your mother? Was too honest to live. That's what it was. She was too honest."

I looked at him and smiled because he was smiling. There we were, smiling about Dead Darla.

But I could picture him then, the way he used to look—cargo shorts and a cut-off flannel shirt and some faded T-shirt that had holes in it. Long, curly hair. Boots. Doc Martens, probably. Young, like Darla was. He was a handsome man. She was a handsome woman. I was their handsome offspring who was also too honest to understand bullshit. And I didn't fit into any conversation I ever heard because all people talked about was dumb crap that I didn't give a shit about. Nobody talked about art. Nobody talked about how the mourning dove lied. Nobody talked about the Zone System.

I fit in here. In my house. In my family, which was just me and Dad since I was four. I didn't think I'd ever fit in anywhere else. Ever. When I looked at Dad, I realized he felt the exact same way. We were mad at the world, and this was the only place it was okay to be mad at the world.

Darla had to escape. That's what she did. So what would I do? What would Dad do? If rolling in bullshit isn't something we can do, then where's the door? There's got to be another door.

"So what did Ellie do this time?" he asked.

"Nothing any worse than what she always does," I said. "She's always about Ellie, you know? Self-serving or whatever."

"But friends forgive each other for that shit, don't they?"

"I don't know," I said. "Ellie has never really been a friend." I felt like the worst person right then. "I mean, we're—uh—accidental friends. She lives there. I live here. But we don't really have much in common or something."

"Huh."

"Is that okay?" I asked.

"Sure. I mean, as long as all this stuff we're talking about isn't turning you away from her. She always seemed like a pretty cool kid."

"But the apple, right? It doesn't fall far and all that."

"Huh," he said again. "But she didn't do anything that made you say that?"

"We had a fight. But it's a fight we should have had years ago, so no, she didn't really do anything specific. Everything serves to further, I guess. You know? Maybe I'm changing. Maybe I'm growing up or maybe she's not. I don't know."

"Be careful with her."

"I'll try." I couldn't explain to him that she hadn't been careful with me.

I walked outside. It was one of those perfect early-June nights. Cool, but I could still wear just a T-shirt. I left all the porch lights off so I could see the stars. I looked up at them and talked to Darla because she was there in the stars because I was there, too. In the history of the world, we are all in the stars, right?

I told her, "Sometimes I want to leave on my own terms too, but I have something to do. I don't know what it is yet, but I know I have something to do."

Transmission from Betelgeuse: *You have something to do.*

Transmission from Vega: *You have something to do.*

Transmission from Polaris: *You have something to do.*

I nearly fell asleep on the porch step, sitting up. Crying was exhausting. I hadn't done it in so long, I'd forgotten how it makes you tired. Maybe Darla was so tired, she just couldn't do it anymore.

Glory O'Brien's History of the Future

Old America will finally gather an army big enough to secure the border. New America will have taken nearly two whole states in nine weeks.

After that initial nine-week assault, Nedrick the Sanctimonious will make more and more public appearances. He will say he has a bigger army in reserve. He will say that all persons over sixty should be euthanized. He will say that all government-funded schools should close and that New America will open its own schools. He will say that women are only good for one thing.

He will not say what that thing is.

New Americans will no longer talk to national network reporters. Nedrick will say, "It's none of their goddamned business."

Girls will begin to disappear from border states at an alarming rate. Twenty to forty per night. The sound of wailing will be as common as the sound of freight trains and traffic.

I don't see where the girls go, but I know enough to guess that they are either sold for money or will end up in a building that has a number on it.

What do you think makes you different?

Dad had the TV on as he worked. I watched him as I ate my granola, still half asleep. Then I said, "Do you have friends anymore? I don't think I ever saw you with friends."

"People suck."

"Not all of them."

"Yeah. Pretty much."

"Right."

"Why?" he asked, looking up over the top of the laptop. Transmission from Dad: *His distant ancestor skewered five of Cromwell's Roundheads with a pike.*

"I don't know," I said. "I don't have any friends either."

"So that stuff about Ellie last night—you were serious?"

"Yeah."

"Just outgrew each other?"

"Exactly," I lied. "I guess."

"Welcome to the rest of your life. It's why I don't bother. Though I might if—"

"If?"

"If I lived somewhere else," he said.

"You think?"

"I don't know. Most guys my age just watch sports and talk about bullshit."

"Everyone talks about bullshit," I said.

"True."

As I chewed the rest of my granola, I realized that the history of the future was not bullshit. It could be complete bat-induced insanity, but it wasn't bullshit. It was showing me something.

Past is future is past is present is future is past is present.

Fact: Past, present and future have one thing in common. Me.

I wished I could take a picture of it. Make it *real*. Make it something I could glue into a sketchbook. More than just some story about what I saw when I looked at people.

Why do people take pictures?

To make things real.

Or real-er.

Or something.

To have memories of things they lost.

To remember—even though sometimes they want to forget.

———

I decided on a day without Ellie. I decided to go to the mall to see if I could find my USS *Pledge* man again. When my phone rang, I answered it without thinking.

"Didn't you get my voice mails?" Ellie asked.

"I was busy," I said.

"Can we go to the mall again?" she asked. [Insert laugh track laughter.]

"Um—I don't know. I—uh—think I have stuff to do here today."

"Liar. You're just avoiding me because I was a bitch yesterday."

"Uh."

"I was. Okay? I was. So let's try it again. I want to see if I can see your war and you probably want to see more too, right?"

"I guess," I said.

"So...I'll be there in five minutes?"

I let a few seconds pass before I answered. "Okay."

I don't know why I said yes. Ellie was a habit. It was early. I didn't have the brainpower to lie to her and tell her I had something else to do.

She arrived on my porch in a new blouse.

"Nice shirt," I said, not commenting on how it was unbuttoned one button too many.

"Thanks."

This was the kind of stuff we said to each other on the way to the mall, too. Small talk, mostly. Then, when we got to the mall, we split up and agreed to meet for lunch at one at the food court.

When I got to the mall, I sat in the center area on one of the benches waiting for my USS *Pledge* man and got as many transmissions as I could.

Transmission from the lady next to me: *Her grandson will discover the gene in humans that carries a rare disease I can't pronounce. His son will then ironically contract the disease and will die and be buried in the same cemetery as Darla's mother. His name will be: Lawrence Julian Harrison. He will live to age nine. His last day in school, he will learn how to multiply fractions. He will never use this skill again in his life.*

Transmission from an old Hispanic man in a pressed Cuban shirt: *His sister's great-grandson will be deported during Nedrick's nine-day assault. After he's deported, his surviving children will become exiles. They will live in the trees and scavenge for food. Seven generations later, his descendants will be invited to be the first inhabitants of the EcoDome on the moon.*

I looked around and tried to meet eyes with someone else and I saw a guy with a trimmed goatee and longish brown hair. He was dressed like Dad used to dress—grunge on a stick. Cut-off flannel, T-shirt, baggy shorts that looked old but not dirty. Boots. A tattoo, a band, around his right arm. He was older than me...but not much older, I don't think. He smiled at me. And he was completely gorgeous.

I felt dumb to think it, but I thought it. His skin was browned like he did a lot of yard work or something. His arms were built, too. I felt wrong noticing these details. As if I was never planning on becoming a sexual being.

I smiled at him.

Transmission from sexy guy who I was trying *not* to compare to young Dad in my head: *He will marry later in life, and he will marry his true love, whom he will meet at the mall one day in June 2014.*

No shit.

I looked away. And then I looked back at him. Transmission from the same guy who might be marrying me at a later date: *He and his wife will run from Ferret Company. The man in the red pickup truck won't be able to catch them. They will destroy many things belonging to the New American Army, including peeling the* MY OTHER TOY HAS TITS *bumper sticker off the red pickup truck. He will be a master of explosives. His wife will be a sharpshooter. He will be eighty-six when he dies in her arms.*

He smiled at me again, so I looked away, but then he sat down on a bench three benches away from me. He had a clipboard. The clipboard made me feel stupid, because up until I saw it, I thought he was smiling at *me*. But he probably just wanted something. When I looked up again, I was face to face with a little girl who was eating a Dum Dum lollipop.

Transmission from the kid with the lollipop: *Her great-grandmother used to tell her stories about surviving the Second World War. They will come in handy when she finds herself living in a swamp to escape the New American Army.*

"Hi," he said—the completely gorgeous guy. I hadn't seen him move. He looked younger now that he was closer. Still older than me. Oh well.

"Hi," I said.

"Peter," he said. He put his hand out, and I shook it. I tried to get a look at what was on his clipboard, but I couldn't see it. Would he ask me for money? A signature? A subscription to a magazine or something?

"I'm Glory." He laughed. They always did. Glory is a porn star name, right? It's a stage name for a lap dancer. "It's short for Gloria," I said, looking at his boots. Doc Martens. Well worn. Oxblood.

"Nice to meet you, Glory," he said.

"Did we meet?" I asked. Then I looked at him again.

Transmission from Peter: *His grandfather was a POW in the Pacific during World War II and had to eat bugs and drink his own urine. His distant descendant will invent a microchip that can be inserted into children that gives them the ability to take standardized tests without fear or boredom.*

"I think we did," he said. "And you have a really pretty smile."

This could have been considered the creepiest conversation that ever took place. If anyone was watching it, they'd have called the police. My dad would run Peter over with his super-market Jazzy. Even Ellie would be grossed out, and she'd slept with Rick-with-crabs-and-books-about-serial-killers.

"That's pretty...creepy," I said. "Nice. But creepy."

He laughed. "Totally didn't come out right."

"That's okay," I said. I focused intensely on his knee. It was also completely gorgeous.

"I'm doing a survey. I've been here every day this week. I'm getting kinda sick of it," he said.

"A survey?" I said. "You're not going to make me answer a bunch of questions, are you?"

"No questions," he said. "You already answered. See?" He showed me a paper clipped into his clipboard that had Xs and a checkmark. "See that checkmark right there? That's you."

The rest of the page was *X*s. Like, fifty of them. "You were like a lighthouse in a storm. That's all. I didn't want to freak you out. I was just happy to find you."

"Why am I the only checkmark?"

"Look around," he said. "What do you think makes you different?"

I looked around. I accidentally made eye contact with a woman walking quickly by. Transmission from woman hurrying by: *Her father was called to Oak Ridge, Tennessee, in 1943 to work on a top secret development called the Manhattan Project. One day, the outcome of the Manhattan Project would be a 9,700-pound bomb named Little Boy.*

I couldn't answer Peter's question right away. *What do you think makes you different?* What made me different was I could see people's infinities. What made me different was that I drank God and had become God. Or I drank a bat and had become a bat. You choose.

What made me different was that I couldn't look you in the eye and just see *you*. Instead, I saw *everything*.

"Well?" he asked.

"What makes me different? Um," I said. I looked around. "I'm not tan and I don't give a crap if I'm tan?"

"Nope."

"I don't dye my hair?"

"Nope."

"Makeup? I don't wear makeup?"

"This isn't just for women," he said. "This is for everyone."

"And you're not going to try and sell me anything?"

"Nope. It's for college."

"You're in college?" I asked. He looked at me and smiled. He knew what I meant. I meant: *Aren't you a little old for college?* I didn't mean to be judgmental. "Sorry."

"It took me a while to figure out what I wanted to be," he said.

"I hear you," I said.

"And I'm only twenty-two."

"Oh," I said.

"So? Any more guesses?"

I shook my head.

"You smiled at me when I smiled at you."

"And?"

"And that's it. You didn't scowl or look down or play with your phone or pretend you didn't see me. You smiled back," he said.

"And this makes me exceptional?"

He moved his hand like the mall population was a prize on a game show. "Try it yourself. This place isn't a hotbed of friendly people."

I wanted to tell him I wasn't friendly. I wanted to tell him I didn't want any friends and didn't have any friends and I wanted to tell him I was happy that way. Except I was too concerned about why I was smiling. That was new. Was it just because a beautiful-looking guy smiled at me first? Had I smiled at other people that day already and not noticed? What was happening to me? I asked, "What are you going to college for?"

"Psychology," he said.

"You here all day?" I asked.

"All day, all week. I'm hungry, though. Will you hold my bench while I run up and get something to eat?"

"Sure."

"You want anything?"

"A taco? Chicken? Extra sour cream."

He gave me a thumbs-up.

I only had my phone camera with me. I'd left my others at home for once. I had an urge to take a picture of him from behind as he walked away. I didn't. But if I had, I'd have called it *All I Did Was Smile*.

That's a high bar

Peter ate sweet-and-sour chicken. He dipped the chicken into the red sauce like it was fast food or something, which was kinda disappointing. I tried to eat the taco, but it was messy while sitting on a bench so I put it back in its little paper tray. But then I decided I didn't care. The guy was a complete stranger. What did he care that I was a slob with tacos, right? He'd brought a hundred napkins, too, so that was good.

We started with small talk about music.

"I love old bands," he said. "Like anything from Zeppelin to Nirvana to the Stones."

"My parents were hippie freaks. I like all of that too. Toss in some Grateful Dead and Hendrix and Pearl Jam and we could be like music twins."

We ate for a while. There was no awkward silence because

my taco was extra crunchy. Or at least it sounded extra crunchy. Every time I looked up at Peter, he got better-looking.

"So you just smile at people all day?" I asked.

He nodded as he chewed.

"Is this, like, a class on how people are dicks or something?"

He laughed a little. "It's a thesis for a summer class. I'm calling it 'The Death of Common Courtesy in the Connected World.'"

"Hmm."

"You ever go online and read comments under articles?"

"I know what you mean, yeah."

"You're in high school, right?"

"Just graduated."

"I'd love to interview you. I mean, about what it's like in high school."

"I thought you were twenty-two," I said. "High school hasn't changed much since you were there."

I chewed the last bite of my taco, which was, like, a third of the entire taco that I'd just shoved in my mouth before it broke into a million pieces all over my lap.

"People in my class say I'm too into this stuff—the idea that humans are becoming less and less interested in other humans and more and more interested in stuff on their computers. That kind of thing."

"I think you're right," I said. "Even friends don't act like friends anymore."

"Meaning?"

"Meaning that friends just text each other or they get together to gossip or look through each other's profiles and they make fun of other people and stuff."

"Have you done that?"

"I don't have any friends," I said.

"I doubt that."

"Doubt all you want. It's true."

He studied me. "Not one friend?"

"I have one. But just because she lives across the road. She's not a very good friend, though. Convenient, I guess."

"You seem cool."

"I am cool."

"So why not have friends?" he asked. "Is it that hard to find other cool people or something?"

"Yes. And no. I don't know. I just don't like people as a rule," I said. "They're very untrustworthy."

"Am I?"

"What?"

"Untrustworthy."

"Maybe."

"I mean, we met less than an hour ago. Doesn't seem like something a misanthrope would do—sit here and eat with a stranger."

"I'm a rebel, I guess."

"So, I'm cool?"

"Yeah. But I don't know you yet," I said. "What usually happens is I get to know someone and then I realize they're not really as cool as they seemed. Or something."

"That's a high bar."

"Nothing wrong with a high bar, right? Why else are you smiling at people all day in the mall?"

"True. But you can't hold everyone up to your expectations."

"Who says?"

"You don't have any friends, right? So, that should be enough proof that it's not working out."

"I don't want any friends," I said. "What about that?"

"You're different," he said. He was smiling, so this was a compliment. Yet I wasn't sure what to say to him. "If you can do that interview, I think you're someone who needs to comment on this for my thesis."

"I thought we were already doing the interview," I said. We both laughed. "So I guess we should talk about music again before it's time for us both to get back to whatever we were supposed to be doing."

"I don't know. I still want to know why you don't want any friends," he said.

I thought about it. "I just don't need them."

"Do you have a close family?"

"Sorta."

"Brothers and sisters?"

"Just me."

"So your parents must be cool, then."

"Yeah. They are."

"So the high bar started at home, eh?"

I laughed. "Yeah. You could say that."

"You're interesting."

"You think?"

"See what I mean?"

"I've never fit in, if that's what you mean," I said. "Not sure if I want to."

"Heh," he grunted. Then he took our empty plates to the trash can. I stood up and when he saw me standing, he looked a little disappointed, as if he wanted to talk more.

"I have to get going," I said.

"Cool. It was nice meeting you," he said. He handed me a card. "So, you're serious? You'll do an interview?"

"Sure. No problem."

"My number is on there. Call me and we'll set it up."

"Okay," I said, only glancing at the card before I put it in my pocket.

"See you soon, then," he said. We shook hands. His handshake was firm. Mine was also firm. We both had high bars.

Transmission from handsome Peter: *His father never liked him and always told him to cut his hair. One time, he told Peter he looked like a faggot.*

———

I smiled at people on my way to the fountain outside Sears. Peter was right. No one smiled back. If anything, the response was the opposite. Smiling at people made them uncomfortable.

I got a few transmissions from passersby and I took notes for *The History of the Future* but I found myself preoccupied by thoughts. Mostly Peter, sometimes the USS *Pledge* guy, but as lunchtime grew nearer, Ellie.

I didn't know what I'd say to her to finally get her out

of my life. She lived across the road, so unless I planned on staying in the darkroom or moving away, it was going to be awkward.

I walked around the usual senior citizen haunts and looked for the USS *Pledge* guy. I even walked around the mall outside—where some people did their daily walk dressed in fashionable workout gear. He wasn't there. He wasn't inside, either.

On my way back into the mall, I passed a flea market–type stand—baseball cards, old vinyl records and other bizarre retro stuff. A pair of sunglasses caught my eye. They were shaped like a bat. The lenses were red. They had little bats that hung on chains as earpieces. I bought them for ten bucks and put them on.

The red glow was part darkroom flashback and part metaphor. I was Glory O'Brien, bat, seeing red. Mad at the world. I was the petrified bat—dead on the inside and fooling you. I was dead to every expectation. Dead to nail polish. Dead to fashion. Dead to celebrity gossip. Dead to what you thought of me. I was free because you would never know me.

Maybe the red lenses made me a little nuts, but that's what I thought.

I am no one special and I am free.

People stared at me in the glasses and I started to feel self-conscious, so I took them off and kept looking for my USS *Pledge* guy.

On my fourth trip around the center of the mall, I started to feel stupid. Maybe the USS *Pledge* guy wasn't even from here. Maybe he'd been visiting a friend or had come to the mall with his daughter or something. It was almost lunchtime. I figured my best chance was the food court. Even though it had only been two hours since I ate the taco with Peter, I was starving.

Cancer enchiladas

On my way to the food court, I looked for Peter, to see if he was still as good-looking as he'd been that morning. Or to see if he was sitting on a bench somewhere asking another girl if he could interview her. The thought had crossed my mind. From the right angle his interview/thesis line could have been something he said to every girl he met at the mall. What did I know?

I didn't find him, but I didn't make a big deal out of it. I was sure he had something to do. I was sure he'd show up somewhere...and he did.

"Who's that?" Ellie asked me while we waited in line for calzones. He'd waved and sat down at the area with the most traffic—presumably to smile at people coming to eat their lunch.

I said, "Peter."

"Where did he come from?"

"I met him this morning," I said. She made a face as if to say she didn't like me meeting anyone.

Ellie and I ate lunch and talked about our transmissions. Ellie periodically looked over at Peter and eye-flirted.

"So? Did you see anything new today?" I asked Ellie.

"I now know that some guy I never met before likes to smell people's shoes when they're not looking. And I know about some woman's grandfather who used to be a tap dancer and I know about some little kid and how her daughter is going to live in the trees."

"Exile," I said. "She's going to live in exile."

"Did you find your wheelchair guy?" Ellie asked.

"I'm hoping he comes to lunch," I answered, then looked around. No wheelchair guy.

Ellie was trying to eat a Styrofoam plate full of hot, radiated enchiladas with a plastic knife and fork. Everything was cancerous. I took a picture of it. *Cancer Enchilada.*

Ellie kept looking at Peter, trying to get his attention. I watched her and realized that I'd thought Ellie was the only person I'd ever have in my life. But in one short morning I'd met a real person who wasn't interested in where I could drive him or what I could buy him at the drugstore. He was just interested in whether I smiled or not. And in what music I liked.

"What's happening to us?" I asked.

"We drank God," Ellie said. "Now we can see everything...including shoe smellers, apparently."

She laughed but I hadn't meant it that way. I meant it in the way she didn't know yet. I meant it to say: *Why are we even pretending anymore?* I said, "Everything is changing."

Ellie looked at Peter again and then looked at me. She said, "His parents live in an over-fifty-five place in Florida and his dad likes to ride his bike a lot. It's green. His mom hates wearing a bathing cap when she uses the community's pool. They have a cat."

Peter looked at me then.

Transmission from Peter: *When his grandmother moved into a nursing home, she was bullied by other residents and combated it by playing jazz piano before breakfast every morning. Peter will do the same thing as an old man during the Second Civil War. He will play harmonica every chance he can to remind fellow rebels that there is good in the world.*

"Holy shit," Ellie said. "He's coming over."

He stopped and said hello. I introduced him to Ellie. Ellie put that pout on her face. I bet if she'd had time, she'd have unbuttoned an extra button on her new blouse.

I asked Peter, "Did she pass your test?"

"Nope," he said.

"What test?" Ellie asked.

"How many checkmarks?"

"Eleven. Finally hit double digits," he said as he waved and walked away.

Ellie looked annoyed that we didn't answer her question. "You should have asked for his number," she said.

I got up to throw my trash away. "I already have it," I said.

I'd be lying if I told you I didn't hope that the future I saw for Peter was also my future. I was hoping that, of all the people he was meeting at the mall during his experiment, I was the one who turned out to be his soul mate in June 2014.

File under: Dumb but true.

File under: I was sick of not living my life.

As Ellie and I made our way down the escalator, she said, "You're still pissed about the other day, aren't you?"

"Not really."

"You are," she said. "You won't even look at me."

"I'm on a fucking escalator, Ellie."

"Well," she said. "Even before now."

I waited until we were down the escalator and out the doors. If we were finally going to have a huge fight, then I wanted enough oxygen to yell as loud as I could.

And I did. "What's your problem?" I asked this in loud, enunciating syllables. Three smoker guys circled around an ashtray/trash can looked over at me.

"What's *your* problem?" she asked back.

I didn't have the energy to go all the way down to her level. The bar was too low.

"All I did was ask if you're still pissed about the other day. You obviously are."

"And I said no. But what I say doesn't seem to matter because you already have all the answers. So why should I even talk to you about it?"

"You are, though," she said. "Right?"

"No."

"So what's with you today?"

I thought about it. "I have shit on my mind, okay? And you've made it very clear that I can't share it with you."

"Like you ever shared anything with me in your life," she said.

"I shared something with you yesterday. And look what happened. Seriously. Why would anyone share shit with someone who's so self-centered?"

She was about to yell something, but then she stopped. "Self-centered?"

"Self-centered."

I started walking to the car. She followed.

"I never really noticed that before," she said. "Being self-centered, you'd think I would have, eh?"

"I guess. I don't know," I said.

"Do you want to go back in? See Peter more? I don't want to make you leave early if you don't want to."

"It's fine. The old guy wasn't there. I'll try another day."

She got in the passenger's-side door when I unlocked it.

"I was kinda hoping to stay out all day," she said. "My mom will just put me to work if I go back." [Insert laugh track laughter.]

I was about to start the car, but I stopped. I looked at her and she frowned. I said, "We can go back in if you want."

"How about somewhere else?" [Insert laugh track laughter.] "Main Street?" Ellie said.

Main Street was the only living street left near our local poverty-eaten city. It was made possible by people who got a revitalization grant. It was a cute, real street where there were stores that didn't have a corporate logo and didn't import everything from China.

So I drove us to Main Street.

And on Main Street, Ellie and I went our separate ways. We agreed to meet back at the car at four. I sat on a fancy-looking bench and smiled at people. Nobody smiled back. I took a small notepad from my purse and started keeping track. An *X* for no smile-backs, a checkmark for smile-backs. I got some transmissions, too.

Transmission from *X* #4: *A distant descendant will open a coffee shop on Jupiter's first space orbiter. He will serve the best chai lattes in the galaxy.*

Transmission from *X* #8: *His father forgot to turn the coffee-maker off this morning and melted the countertop in his condo.*

Transmission from *X* #14: *His grandson will rob a bank in Mt. Pitts, Pennsylvania, and will spend nine years in prison for it. His other grandson will attempt to abduct a seven-year-old girl and will go to the same prison for three months before he is released. That grandson will euthanize his grandfather so he can have his car, a 1997 Dodge Neon with no air-conditioning and low mileage.*

Transmission from *X* #19: *His ancient ancestor fought in the Mongol invasion of Iraq in the thirteenth century. He fired arrows from a crossbow and killed seven people with his bare hands.*

Transmission from *X* #24: *Her great-granddaughter will be exiled after the Fathers Count Law is passed. She will join the rest of the exiles—all single mothers—and form a community that lives deep in the forests east of their suburb.*

Transmission from my only checkmark, a woman in her twenties with a really cool tattoo on her clavicle: *She will join the revolution and take food to the forests. She will lead many to safety. She will lose both of her daughters to the machine. She will eventually become my best friend.*

I smiled back at her smile. She slowed as we looked at each other. I already liked her. I already wanted to hang out with her more than I wanted to hang out with Ellie.

She made me see the possibilities.

Fact: There are so many people in the world.

Why was I hanging out with one I didn't really like?

Was everyone stuck with geographical friends like this? Longitude-and-latitude friends?

I sat on the nearest bench and looked at my paper. Thirty-four *X*s and one checkmark. My cheeks hurt from smiling so much. Or maybe they were fatigued because so few smiled back.

Peter must have been exhausted. I took a phone picture of my tally and sent it to him on his cell phone number, which I found on his card. I didn't want to get too familiar. I just thought he might want to know that he inspired me. Maybe smiling at people would be my new revenge on the bullshit world.

Maybe smiling at people would be my cure for mother-in-the-oven.

Would we care more?

Smiling at people put me in zone, like, 9. It was true what they said about it having a psychological effect on a person. I was happier because I smiled ... not the other way around.

Ellie found me on my bench and sat down.

"I've stopped caring," she said.

"About what?"

"About the transmissions."

"Okay," I said.

"I just want it to go away now."

"Yeah. It will. Don't worry."

"Why do you sound so sure?"

"I don't know."

Silence.

"I'm sorry I'm self-centered," she said.

"I'm sorry you are, too."

"I thought about it and I guess I make a pretty bad friend."

I didn't want her to feel bad. We had enough going on. So I lied. "You're not that bad," I said.

"Let's just go home."

I agreed and we walked to the car.

"My mom is throwing another star party tomorrow night," she said.

"That's quick," I said. "Two in one week?"

"Something about the planets," she said, pretending to be disinterested in the planets.

I thought about what Jasmine's parties might have been like back when Darla and Dad were probably doing psychedelic mushrooms and knew pornographers and stuff.

Not to say I cared what other people did with their time or their bodies. I couldn't have cared less if Jasmine liked to swing naked by her hair from a tree while every one of the commune dwellers tossed live rodents at her.

What I *did* care about was how young Rick must have been when he started impregnating women on the commune. It made me wonder, if Rick was a girl, would we care more? Would there be a court-approved name for what women on the commune were doing with him? Would we shame him for teenage pregnancy? Could we? In a world that screamed *Be Sexy or Just Die Now*, could we really blame him?

"Did you hear me?" Ellie said.

"Oh. Yeah. Sorry. I was thinking about something else."

"That Peter guy, right?"

"Ew. No."

"Um, do you have eyes?"

"I didn't mean he's not hot. He's hot. But he's too old for me, you know?"

"I guess," she said.

"So the party. I can't make it tonight," I said.

"It's tomorrow night."

Shit. "Oh."

"Markus Glenn is coming. He's going to pretend like he's my boyfriend so Rick gets jealous," she said.

"Markus Glenn the porn kid? How did you even see him?"

"He was running. Up our road. Saw me and we talked. That's all."

"You'd make a cute couple," I said.

"Stop. That's not why he's coming. I told you." She sighed. "I wish I could go back to last Saturday and not drink the bat," she said. I found it strange that she chose to blame the bat. Sleeping with Rick was long before the bat.

"I thought you thought it was cool. I mean, a little, at least. Right? Clan of the petrified bat and all that?"

"Meh. I don't want to even look at my parents anymore, you know?"

"I saw my dad's ancestors eating a big fucking deer. It was weird."

"Yeah. My mom mustn't have been married to my dad yet. She was naked. I don't want to talk about it."

So we'd both seen Jasmine Blue naked. And neither of us wanted to talk about it. I reached for my door handle to get out and she said, "Glory?"

"Yeah?"

"Are you sure we're gonna be okay?"

"Sure."

"I mean you and me?"

Fact: I was sure we were not going to be friends a year from now. But I lied. "I think so. I don't know."

"The war you're seeing. It scares me."

"It's in here," I said, tapping myself on my skull. "How can we be scared of something if we're not sure it's really going to happen?" She nodded. "Plus, if it is true, you're going to have kids and then get to be a grandmother. You need to forget all this war stuff. Just leave it to me."

"I wonder if Nostradamus drank a petrified bat before he saw all that shit," she said.

She came around to my side when she got out and hugged me like she needed a hug, but I couldn't find the love to hug her back. I fake-hugged her. All I wanted to do was get to my darkroom.

My darkroom. Not Darla's. Darla wrote *Why People Take Pictures*. I was writing *The History of the Future*. Darla took pictures of her dead tooth and tree stumps. I took pictures of things that were empty. We were a diptych. Mother-and-daughter diptych. She killed things, and I showed the hole that followed.

"See you later?" Ellie said. "After dinner?"

"I'm doing something with Dad tonight," I said. "He felt bad for not taking me out for graduation."

"Cool. Tomorrow, then. I'll come over in the morning."
[Insert laugh track laughter.]

She crossed the road and walked toward the commune. I stood there and marveled at it—the farmhouse especially, with the thick limestone and the slate roof. I took a picture. I called the picture: *Mine.*

Then I turned the camera toward myself and took about five shots of me in my new bat glasses. I sneered. The caption would read: *Glory O'Brien, Mad at the World.*

———

Dad said he wanted us to go out for dinner to my favorite Mexican restaurant. I didn't tell him I'd planned on spending the evening in the darkroom printing, reading and writing the history of the future. I wanted to tell him. Of all the people, he was the one who might understand it. He looked like a guy who'd done psychedelic mushrooms at least once.

I asked him at dinner.

"Did you ever do psychedelic mushrooms?"

He shook his head at first, the way people do when they want to say *Geez, kid, that's some question.* Then he said, "Sure. A bunch of times. It was—"

"The nineties," I answered. "Yeah. I know."

"Have you?" he asked.

"Nah."

We ordered three plates of food and ate like starving people.

"This is nice," I said.

"Yeah."

"For once you don't look like you want to run out of here because of all the people."

"Oh good. So I'm hiding it well?"

We laughed. I watched him and I thought about Peter. I had this strong feeling that they would meet one day. Or that could have been me hoping I was the girl of Peter's dreams. Whatever it was, I wanted Dad to meet him. Maybe they could be friends. Peter didn't talk about bullshit. I bet Dad would like him a lot.

Day one of knowing a handsome guy and I was daydreaming all this. I rolled my eyes at myself internally. *Jesus. You're as bad as Ellie.*

Glory O'Brien's
History of the Future

Nedrick the Sanctimonious will make mistakes. He will forget that blowing people up makes them stronger. Eventually.

While his army is mired in one battle for months, he will neglect his flock in New America. They will begin to sabotage because life isn't so great anymore without basic services and exiled loved ones. Hundreds of tons of ammunition will explode and three of his training camps will fall. He will blame the rebels. He will look for a list of leaders. The name O'Brien will be at the top of that list.

But his intelligence leaders will tell him the truth. He will deliver a speech calling his own people traitors. They will riot in all seceded states. A story will come out of his headquarters about the night he discovers this betrayal. He will be quoted. "Like any good father, I will discipline my children."

This will be when K-Duty turns on its own. Entire towns in New America will become camps. Making soldiers will become a factory process.

While Nedrick still headlines as a man with many followers, he will be alone in the world.

The only friend he will have left will be the man in the red pickup truck.

Innocence sells

I sat in the darkroom and read the rest of *Why People Take Pictures*. It wasn't that hard because I'd already read most of it. Except for one last journal-like entry, which was written below a Polaroid picture of a dead firefly.

> *Last night I couldn't sleep. There was a lightning bug in our room. I watched him for an hour until I got up and went to the bathroom for a pee and he followed me.*
>
> *Let me tell you about our toothbrush.*
>
> *It's rechargeable and Roy mounted it on the wall next to the socket. When it charges, a funky blue light blinks. And do you know what happened?*
>
> *The lightning bug made love to my toothbrush.*
>
> *I stood and watched it dance first, three blinks, then none, hover, three more blinks, and then it landed right*

*on the handle of the toothbrush and mated. It was two
in the morning and I didn't know what to say. I didn't
know what to do. I watched as long as I could and then
sat on the toilet seat, depressed. Because this is us. This is
us, and I hate that this is us, and this is you, and this is me,
and this is the whole fucking world who can afford to be
us. We are natural, beautiful, magical creatures humping
flashy machines.*

I turned to the last of Darla's pictures. It was a Polaroid of our house. The sun must have been setting, because the windows were a warm orange and the siding seemed yellow. It looked void of her somehow—as if Darla already knew that this would be the last picture she'd take of our house.

I paged back to her *You're a pornographer too, you know* page and I looked closely at the tub of anti-aging cream she had taped there. It was a great picture. She'd somehow made the tub look sinister. The background was shadow, but not black. Just a weird evil shadow. Like something—in this case, wrinkles—might jump out at you and bite you when you were least expecting it.

I paged back to the pictures of the porn women. *You. Are. All. Worth. More. Than. This.* Each one struck a common pose—the poses I'd seen since I was a child. Suck in belly, push out chest. Flex calves, high-heeled tippy-toes. Let your knees fall out just a little. Pout. Bite your lip. Look innocent.

Look innocent.

Look innocent.

Because no matter what age you are, looking innocent is sexy. And looking sexy is *everything*. I couldn't think of any pictures I'd seen lately of women who were just *there* and not trying to look sexy.

Then I remembered one.

The donation box at the drugstore, for the local lunch lady who has ovarian cancer and can't pay her medical bills. There was a picture of her sitting in a chair that looked enormous because she'd shrunk so small. She was bald. She was smiling.

But she wasn't trying to look sexy.

She wasn't sucking in or pushing out because she was too busy dying. She was no one special and she was dying. And we were no one special and we were sexily dropping a few coins into her donation box as we paid for our wrinkle cream at the drugstore.

Shit.

We were all fireflies humping toothbrushes.

No wonder Darla was mad at the world.

I opened up my sketchbook. I answered Darla.

We are natural, beautiful, magical creatures who are so busy being sexy we forget that fireflies are sexier than we are. I have never made love to anything, yet. I don't know if I ever will. But I will not make love to a toothbrush. I promise.

I felt like a ghost

I decided I might give Ellie a chance. I'd never shared anything with her. I'd never told her my biggest fear. My biggest secret.

Maybe I was choosing to be lonely.

I decided, since it was only eight thirty, that I should go over to the commune and find her and tell her I was mad at the world. Maybe if we could start there, I could eventually tell her the truth about me.

I saw the lights on in the chicken house, so I walked there to find her. I brought a blanket so we could go and sit in the field and talk. I brought a bag of contraband snacks inside the blanket. Doritos. Fluorescent orange. Our favorite.

When I got to the chicken house, all I found was one of the preteen girls who sometimes helped Ellie with her chores cleaning out the duck pen. I think her name was Matilda.

"Is Ellie around?" I asked.

"She's out in the field."

"Oh," I said. "Thanks."

Matilda went back to the chickens. I fast-walked to the back field.

And before I got all the way there, I saw something I never wanted to see.

Ellie on top of Markus Glenn—the boy from down the road who once asked me to touch his tipi.

I stopped dead.

I slowly turned around so they wouldn't see me, but before I could get far enough away, I heard Ellie yelling. "Glory! Come back!"

But I kept walking.

I wasn't jealous.

I wasn't mad at them. I was mad at the world.

Why shouldn't I be mad at the world? The world let fire-flies hump toothbrushes. The world was so full of shit.

"Glory!" Ellie yelled. "Stop! Wait!"

I didn't turn around. I didn't want to talk to Ellie about anything right then. I knew what was going to happen to her grandsons. They would be slaves to the machine—fingers that reached out in the night and stole lives.

Next thing I knew, she was grabbing my shoulder from behind. "Seriously. Would you stop, please?"

I stopped and turned around. The Doritos fell out of my blanket.

"What?" she said.

I didn't say anything.

"You told me we'd make a cute couple," she said.

I didn't say anything.

"So what's your problem?"

I thought about this. "I'm mad at the world," I said.

"Shit," she answered.

"I came over to talk to you about it," I said. "And Matilda told me you were in the field. I didn't expect you to be screwing him...but I guess you move fast."

She crossed her arms and started to cry a little. Her dress was hanging crooked and I wondered if she had underwear on. I don't know why I wondered that, but maybe that's what I was supposed to wonder.

"I'm not mad at you," I said. "I was just coming to talk to you about something else and I didn't expect to see that. That's all."

The silence wasn't awkward then. It was just silent.

"I'm ready for it to go away now," she said. "All of it."

"Me too," I said. We were such cowards. There we were on a speeding train, and instead of putting our heads out the window and screaming *wheeeeeeeee*, we complained.

We stood there on the edge of the road for a few seconds and listened to an approaching car, and then saw its lights and then watched it pass us, the kids in the backseat staring as if we were ghosts.

I felt like a ghost.

Ellie probably did, too.

Ellie sighed and started to cry. "You totally think I'm a slut."

"I don't." I did. I totally did think she was a slut. It made me cry.

She looked at me. "Why are *you* crying?"

I shook my head. "I'm mad at the world," I said. "Go back," I said, pointing to the field. "Have a good night."

"But what about you?" she said.

"I'll see you in the morning," I said. "Remember?"

She nodded and turned toward the field. As I watched her walk away I thought about Peter and how she flirted. She'd flirted with everyone that way since I could remember.

It wasn't just her. All the girls in school did, too.

Somehow, Darla doing what she did saved me from this. As I walked back to the porch, I was thankful. I'd been so preoccupied with whether or not I would turn into Darla—so busy being the walking picture of emptiness—that I'd over-looked society's expectations of me.

I smiled at this.

Did all outcasts come to this realization at a certain point in life? That being outcast from a bogus and pornographic society actually was a good thing? I hoped so. I hoped there was an army of us out there, smiling about it that very moment.

I'm not normal

I got up at dawn again. I hadn't been sleeping past six. Habit, I guess.

I sat on the front porch and looked over at the commune. *My commune.* It wasn't that I was greedy or that I wanted to hurt Jasmine or Ellie or any of the commune families by taking it back. Maybe part of me wanted to hurt Jasmine for what she did to Dad and Darla, but it was more logical than that.

It was our land.

I thought, for our sake, we should have it.

If Dad wanted to move to California or Vermont, then he'd need it. If he died tomorrow, then I would be left with the mess. I didn't care if Ellie never spoke to me again. I didn't care if Jasmine threw a hissy fit. It was ours. The trick would be convincing Dad, who had been happy to leave things the way they were in order to avoid having to do anything about it. Probably reminded him of what happened. Probably reminded him of everything.

Ellie saw me on the porch and walked over at around eight.

"I'll be back at nine. Is that okay? Extra chores for missing yesterday. My mother is a freak."

"I don't feel like it today, Ellie," I said.

"Why not?"

"I just want to be by myself today or something," I said. As I said it, I could see her processing the last time we saw each other. I hoped she would remember that I was mad at the world. I hoped she might ask me if I was okay.

"It's Markus, isn't it?"

I stayed silent.

"God, Glory. What is *wrong* with me? Why can't I just be a normal girl like you are?"

"I'm not normal," I said.

"You're what my mom wants me to be," she said.

"Your mom doesn't like me," I said. "Because I look like my mom."

"We both look like our moms," she said. "Shit. I hope that doesn't mean we're going to do what they did."

"Like what?"

"Like break up," she said. "I don't want to break up."

"I don't think we will," I said. "I mean, the thing that broke them up was kind of a big deal, and that can't happen to us."

"What was that?" Ellie asked.

"What?"

"The thing that broke them up?"

Since I couldn't tell Ellie the truth, I said the first thing that came to mind. "The land."

She cocked her head. "What land?"

"Where you live. The commune. It's my mom's land," I said, pointing to her house.

"So they fought over the price of it or something?"

"Well, no," I answered. "They never bought it from her. It's—uh—still ours, pretty much."

"What?"

"The land."

"It's still yours? Like we rent?" she said.

"No rent."

I think she was mad, but not as mad as she would have been had I told her the real reason that our mothers stopped talking to each other.

We stayed there for a minute, just looking over at her house. She was processing, probably. I was still wondering if she'd ever ask me if I was okay. She didn't, so I changed the subject.

"So what's the deal with you and Markus Glenn?" I asked. "Has he gotten any less assholey since seventh grade?"

"He was—um—kinda weird with me last night," she said.

"Like how?"

"He was pretty pervy."

I laughed a little. "You didn't know this?"

"Well, yeah, but I mean, he wouldn't even kiss me. He just kept—you know—paying attention to my boobs."

"Paying attention? That's romantic."

She smacked me on my arm. "It's not funny. It was kinda creepy, pretty much. It was like the rest of me didn't really exist. Just—uh—them."

"Your boobs."

"Yeah."

I sighed. "He's probably watched so much boob porn that boobs are like people to him now or something."

"Yeah."

"Did he call them by name?" I asked, giggling.

She laughed. "Stop it."

"But did he?"

"He's still coming to the star party tonight."

I didn't question her motives or her sanity. Maybe this is what normal girls do, right? And I did what other normal girls do. There are billions of us out there. Just like stars—none of us is the same.

"I'm still invited, right?" I said.

"Of course," she said.

She went back to the commune and I watched her walking and I wondered how many times Darla sat on this porch and watched Jasmine walk back to the commune. I wondered if Darla ever wanted to take it back, too.

———

The Zone System didn't have a zone for how I was feeling right then. I was very high contrast—all blacks and whites and no grays. I was a lithograph.

My zone 0 was max black: *Holy shit I am living next door to a bunch of sex-crazed freaks and my mother killed herself after one of the sex-crazed freaks sent naked pictures of herself to my father. Or, in short: I am an extra in an ugly movie about sex-crazed squatter hippies. I didn't sign up for this shit.*

My zone 10 was blown-out white: *I am probably the sanest person I know, even though my mother killed herself when I was four, I eat all microwaved food and I live across the road from squatter hippies. Compared to my sex-crazed friend, I am a real winner.*

I went inside and took a long shower. After my shower, I curled up in bed and tried to take a nap. Instead, I thought about the transmissions and how a day without them would be better than a day at the mall with Ellie. Even if I missed a chance to see Peter. Even if I missed a chance to find my USS *Pledge* man, who might have the answers I'd been looking for.

After an hour under my covers not sleeping, I got up and got dressed and wrote a chapter in my book about some of the transmissions I'd seen in the mall the day before. Then I opened my computer and waited for it to boot up.

I wanted to look up the USS *Pledge*.

I wanted to look up squatters' laws in Pennsylvania.

Glory O'Brien's History of the Future

Ferret Company will fail. Night after night, the man in the red pickup truck will return to headquarters and tell Nedrick the Sanctimonious that exile forest camps are empty. They will not know about the tunnels.

While Nedrick tries to maintain his failing campaign, his New America will crumble. Breeding camps will fall mere months after being established, residents burning them as they escape. The New American Army will be divided. Some will follow because they are frightened. Some will defect. Some will be murdered by the Sniper.

The Sniper will know where to find them—in groups. She will know of their meetings and their hideouts. She will arrive in just the right spot behind enemy lines from underground.

The exiles will have decided, after years in the trees, that tunneling is their only hope. Or their downfall. They won't be sure. But they have nothing to lose, so they will dig.

The Sniper looks familiar to me from the back. She wears boots that have a hole in the right sole. She usually has dirt all over her. She's intriguing.

Minesweeper

So, the USS *Pledge* was one of two minesweeper ships. It was either one that sank during the Korean War or it was one that fought in the Vietnam War and was eventually sold to Taiwan in 1994 for $21,263.80.

When I looked up squatters' rights, I didn't plan on finding anything. I'd only ever heard the term referring to abandoned houses in the city. Crack houses, mostly. But I learned that squatters' rights do exist in Pennsylvania. If a person lives on or uses land for twenty-one years without being served a legal document from the owner, then they can put in a claim and can, in a court, be awarded the land.

Jasmine Blue Heffner was smart. She was probably writing her claim to my land as I sat in my room writing the history of the future and reading about naval ships. But from what I read, all Dad had to do was send her a registered letter to let her know that he knew she was trespassing and she couldn't take the land from us.

And so I wrote the letter right then.

I used an online example.

Dear Jasmine Blue Heffner, You are trespassing on my land at 33 Blue Pond Way and have been since June 1995. If you do not cease and desist I will file a trespassing action against you. Love, Glory O'Brien.

I printed the letter, folded it, and put it on my desk where the fifty-thousand-dollar check had lain only days before.

––––––––

Ellie came over after lunch. I told her I was going to the library that afternoon to research the first Civil War and figure out how we might be able to stop the second one. This was a lie in case she wanted to hang out. I was really great at lying to Ellie now. I didn't even have to look away.

"Why are you so interested in this war, anyway? It's all in our heads, you know. It's all made-up crazy shit from the petrified bat."

"I don't know," I answered. "I guess I'm not sure."

"You're not sure the hallucinations we've had since we drank a dead bat are real?"

"Some of the stuff I've seen is real."

"Like what?"

"Most of the past stuff. Like my dad's family and history. And Rick—you know. The kids. And all kinds of shit has been real."

"But the future stuff could be bogus."

"Why would it be?"

"Why wouldn't it be?" she asked, snarkily.

"Is there a problem?" I asked. "Because I'm pretty sure everything was fine this morning and now you're acting like I'm a big pain in your ass and you know, that's fine, but if you could just say it, that would be better."

She took a dramatic breath. "Sorry."

"So?"

She breathed dramatically again. "That thing you told me before. About us not paying you rent. Is that really true?"

"Yeah."

"We're just, like, freeloading?"

"I guess. I'm not sure what that means," I said. "I mean, I know what *freeloading* means, but I'm not sure what the arrangement was. It's probably nothing to worry about."

"Shit. Your mom must have been a nice lady to give all that to Jasmine," she said. "She never talks about it, you know."

My brain said, *I'm sure she doesn't.* My mouth just stayed quiet.

"It must be hard to lose someone like you guys lost her," she said.

I was glad she said it. Finally. But I also knew it took her until we were seventeen to say it, and that was the best she could do. I decided to end it right there. In my head, we were no longer friends. We could appreciate the years we had. We could appreciate our past. But she wouldn't be in my future. I had control over that.

Free yourself. Have the courage. You know?

Past doesn't always have to be the present.

Present doesn't always have to be the future.

Beer

Once Ellie left, I went inside and flopped myself on the big green chair across from the couch and watched Dad working. He muttered to himself about dumb callers and celebrated when he got a client off a call. He winked at me a few times. The air-conditioning was cranked to ARCTIC.

"You need me, Cupcake?"

"Only when you have a second," I said.

He typed in some stuff and said, "Once I get this woman her link, we'll be good to go."

"Cool."

I had my *History of the Future* book with me and reread my chapter about the Sniper that I'd written that morning. I was still intrigued. Something about her made me think she would be the one in the tunnel with the USS *Pledge* guy's descendant. Maybe she'd be my daughter or my granddaughter or something.

"Everything all right?" he asked, still waiting for a beep from his computer to say that the client was gone.

"Yeah. Just a few more questions," I said.

He didn't look scared this time. The last two times, he was scared.

Maybe the talking was helping him, too. We *had* waited thirteen years.

When he was done sending the link and the beep sounded, he put his computer down, got up and grabbed himself a microwaved burrito and a small bowl of tortilla chips and sour cream. He also grabbed a beer.

He didn't ever drink beer.

I was so shocked I said, "Beer?"

He chewed on his sour cream–dipped burrito and said, "You told me I should try new things."

"Did I?" I remembered telling him I wanted him to paint again. I didn't remember anything about beer.

"You don't want one, do you?"

Beer reminded me of last Saturday night and the bat. I would probably never drink it again. "No thanks."

"So what's up?" he said. "UPS man brought your darkroom stuff today." He pointed to the once–dining room table. "I got you three sizes of paper. I wasn't sure if you wanted to go to sixteen by twenty or not, but what the hell, right?"

"Thanks," I said. And then I went into my pocket and got the letter. "I did some research today. I think you need to know about this." I handed him the letter and he started reading it. "If we don't send her a letter now, she could take the land from us. I don't think we should let her have it. I don't care if it breaks me and Ellie up."

He finished reading it and then he read it again. I could see his reading eyes start back at the top left of the paper.

"Obviously, you'd have to sign it," I said. "It's not my land."

"Shit, kid. I can't do this."

I gave him the *WTF?* face.

"I hate confrontation. I hate Jasmine. Mixing the two is just too much. I mean, for me, you know?"

"They can take the whole place from you. The house, the land, the barn. All of it. Like—not too long from now, either. Maybe a year? Whatever is twenty-one years from when you gave it to them."

He turned this over in his head and made a few grunty noises in his throat. "I'll think about it," he said, and he dropped the letter onto his lap.

I just looked at him. He was sloppy. Clearly, one beer was his limit.

"I don't get why you're afraid of her," I said.

He shook his head. "I'm not afraid of her," he said. "It's her home. It's where she raised her kid. I mean, how would I feel if someone took this place away from me? I couldn't do that to another person."

"You paid for this place," I said.

"Your mother paid for it. I didn't have a pot to piss in."

"So then sign the deeds over to me and I'll kick her ass off," I said.

He eyed me suspiciously.

I eyed him suspiciously.

"Is something going on between you and Ellie? Is she getting on your nerves or something? You can just ignore her, like I ignore them all. You don't have to hurt anybody," he said.

"I don't want to hurt anybody. I just want what's ours. It's important."

Dad frowned. "I didn't raise you to think like that."

"California, remember? The Virgin Islands?" I said. "You can't sell this place without taking the land back." I looked around the room. I saw the art. The TV. The couch. His tie-dyed T-shirt. I saw the new darkroom supplies on the table, waiting to be exposed and developed. "I want us to get on with our lives, Dad. I want us to be what Mom would have wanted us to be. You painting, me growing up and having a life. Not stuck in neutral. Not just sitting around eating microwave dinners," I said. "I want to go to college. I want to *be* somebody. I want to *do cool shit*."

He stared at me and looked a bit shocked. Or happy. Or thoughtful.

"So think about it, okay?" I pointed to the letter on his lap. "I know it seems wrong. I know it seems..."

"Vindictive?"

"Yeah. But it's not. It's not even mean. Do you know what's mean? Squatting on someone else's land for nineteen years and never even thanking them for it. What's mean is knowing you can steal it if you wait them out. That's mean. This is hard and seems mean, but it's not mean."

"It's a lot of things."

"Just think about it," I said.

"Okay."

I took my new boxes of paper to the darkroom and I didn't print anything. I just sat there on a stool and looked around. I looked at the tooth and I wanted to touch it, for some reason. It was part of Darla. I could tell it things. It could keep me strong as I wrote another entry in *The History of the Future*.

I stood on the stool and untacked it from the ceiling and when I sat back down, I took off the message—*Not living your life is just like killing yourself, only it takes longer*—and I tacked that to the door. I cupped the tooth in my hands. Someone had drilled a tiny hole through the tooth and strung the red thread through it. The roots were long and chunky and ugly.

All the rest of her had been cremated and saved for Dad's ashes so they could be scattered together in the Caribbean Sea, where they'd honeymooned. I didn't have anywhere to visit when I felt like crying about it. I didn't have a gravestone to hug or a place to leave flowers. So I held the tooth and had an imaginary conversation with Darla.

ME: Why shouldn't I kick them off the land?

DARLA: Because then Jasmine would win.

ME: What would Jasmine win?

DARLA: She'd be the ultimate nonconsumerist. She'd be the ultimate hippie.

ME: Are you fucking kidding me?

DARLA: No.

ME: She's a parasite, Mom.

DARLA: She's a very smart parasite, then.

I went back upstairs and flopped on the green chair again. Dad looked up from his laptop.

"Is this some endurance test of hippieness? Like, if you ask for your own land back, that will be you being a consumerist and she will win or some shit?"

He cocked his head. "A little bit, yeah."

I looked at him. First, I wondered if the imaginary conversation I'd just had with Darla was really Darla. I was pretty sure it wasn't. I just think like Darla.

Oh well.

Then I got a transmission from Dad.

He will be a very old man when he dies. I will be with him. I will be pretty old too. He will hug me and tell me he's proud of what I've done. I will be wearing a headband.

This was huge. It nearly made me cry on the spot. *I was going to grow old? Like old-old?*

The headband thing bothered me. It looked like I was wearing it as a bandage, not as a fashion accessory.

"You're looking at me like I'm crazy," Dad said.

"You *are* crazy."

He shook his head.

"I read all about that law this morning," I said. "She's going to win everything. The land, the house, the barn. After all that, she'll finally have you, like she always wanted you. I don't think Mom would be happy about that at all. Consumerist or nonconsumerist."

"I gotta get back to work," he said.

I went back to my room and I opened my sketchbook.

I paged to *Empty Jar*.

I asked myself, "What will you put in your jar, Glory?"

Glory O'Brien's History of the Future

The Sniper will almost kill Nedrick the Sanctimonious twice. Once as he drives in his best friend's red pickup truck. And the second time, it will be near his home, and he will send dogs in the direction of the shot.

The Sniper will make it out alive, but the dogs will discover the tunnel.

During the next week, the government's army will take back most of its states and the residents will be happy. They will be freed from the camps. Children will be reunited with their mothers. Wives will be reunited with their husbands.

Ferret Company will be dismantled. K-Duty will cease. All able-bodied New American men will be commanded to report to the last state ruled by Nedrick the Sanctimonious and will amass for one final battle, which they know they will lose, but they will do it anyway.

Exiles will start the long walk home. They will look like ghosts— withered by three years of hunger and war. The children will stay chillingly quiet. The Sniper will hide in the tunnels with her rebels. Her husband will plant explosives under enemy territory. She will clean her rifle. They will wait in silence as troops march above their heads. They will wait until the right moment. Until they are sure.

How's Glory?

Ellie called me at six that night and said she needed my help with the chickens because she didn't have enough time and she'd miss going to her own star party if she didn't get her chores done. [Insert laugh track laughter.] I'd been napping, so her call annoyed me, but I got up eventually and walked across the road and marveled at the sunset.

Some people think all sunsets are colorful, but they aren't. Some sunsets are more colorful than others. This one was particularly colorful. It started with the blue sky, changed to green and then purple and then pink and then orange and deep red just over the horizon. It might have been the most colorful sunset I ever saw.

I did not know it would be the last sunset I saw as Max Black the bat.

But maybe that made it what it was.

I ran into Jasmine first.

"How's Glory?" she asked.

I looked at her. Right through her. "Glory is awesome. How's Jasmine?"

She seemed surprised at my confidence. "Jasmine is just great," she said. "But she has to go and unlock the drum shed."

They had a shed for drums. Surely a nonconsumerist drum shed would be *not a drum shed and no drums because they are possessions and all possessions are bad*? Maybe I needed to reexamine what *nonconsumerist* really meant. Or maybe Jasmine did.

When I found Ellie, she was already done cleaning out the chicken pen. She laid down wood shavings and mixed a pile of them with straw and then she spread the whole pile out on the floor and sprinkled it with some weird powder that helps chickens not have mites.

Communes. The ripest place in the world for parasites, I guess.

As we walked toward her house I noticed that the star party didn't even seem to be set up yet—no tables, no stools. Not even a fire.

Ellie and I washed our hands in the outdoor sink and she said she had to go inside for a minute and asked me to wait.

Rick walked up to me as I was drying my hands on my shorts.

"She says she has a boyfriend," he said. "Jasmine won't like that."

"Jasmine? Or you?" I asked.

Then I looked at him. Transmission from Rick: *His grand-father was on board the USS* Pledge *when it hit a mine and then sank in Wonsan Harbor, Korea, in 1950. He and his shipmates were rescued by another boat, but he'd been in the wrong part of the ship when the mine hit and he'd taken a huge chunk of steel into his backside. By the time he was released from the VA hospital back home, he'd gotten the last rites twice, been told he'd lose both legs, and was prepped for a short life in a wheelchair before a certain death from an infection he couldn't kick. The man would live for seventy-four more years, until he was ninety-three years old. He would love the calzones they made in the food court at the local mall.*

BOOK FOUR

Remnants of the future

The process of growing up is a little like being on a runaway train. There is nothing you can do about it once it starts, and it starts when you're born. The bat had no say in the matter. We had no say in the matter. You have no say in the matter.

Who knew?

Ellie came out of her house, glared at Rick, who walked away
the minute she did, and asked, "Do you have a minute?"

"I'm here, aren't I?" I looked around. We seemed to be the
only ones there. The drum shed's doors were closed. Lights
seemed to be on in most of the RVs out back. Maybe Jasmine
had called off the star party. I looked at the sky. Clear. I looked
back at Ellie.

"I need to talk to you about something important," Ellie
whispered.

"Okay," I whispered back.

"Not here," she whispered. "It's not safe to talk about it
here."

"There's no one here, though."

"They're here. They're always here."

"Oh," I said.

"Can we go to your house?"

She'd already started walking toward my house, so I followed her. When I'd have gone to the back door, she went to the front, which was rare. We never used the front door.

She didn't knock or anything. Just walked in. And in that split second, I saw her as Jasmine—taking property and not even thinking about it, even if that property was your husband.

And then the sound of too many people yelling "Surprise!" kinda knocked me into the doorjamb. Ellie yelled it the loudest.

Aunt Amy was there in the forefront and opened her arms to me and as I hugged her, I saw that there were balloons and streamers and all sorts of party things that had never been seen inside our house before.

Also, Jasmine was there. And Ed Heffner. And Rick. (And who knew how many Jupiterians.) And probably every member of the yearbook club. And Stacy Cullen brought a bunch of my first-grade friends and there were two kids I shared homeroom with. Strangers. But strangers who were in my house.

"Wow," I said.

That's all I said.

So I said it again. "Wow."

Then I saw Dad, who had managed to put on a pair of real shorts, and he smiled at me and looked pained and all sorts of mixed up about everything I was pained and mixed up about too.

Mostly, I think we were freaked out that Jasmine Blue Heffner was in our house.

Aunt Amy said something like "I can't believe you gradu-ated!" or "We're so proud of you!" or "Time moves so fast!" It all rolled into one. She was nicer than I remembered her. Still wobbling her silicone cleavage around, but who cares?

Transmission from Aunt Amy: *Her son will marry a Jew-ish girl and convert, and Aunt Amy won't care one bit.*

She said, "Did you see your cake?" and pointed to a cake.

"Who did this?" I asked, looking at Dad, who was creep-ing through the strangers to give me a hug. No transmis-sion from Dad because I was focusing on his forehead—a transmission-free night. I hoped.

"It wasn't me, Cupcake," he said. "You told me not to, remember?"

I wanted to say, *And I told you not to for a reason. Watch out if any of those commune people use the bathroom or sit on the couch.*

"Ellie did it, mostly," Aunt Amy said. "I called her and she told me who to call and—" *Ding dong.*

Dad answered the door. It was two more kids from school; one was Stacy Cullen's boyfriend and the other was his friend. I heard him whisper, "Is there beer?"

Ellie was over in the corner of the living room with Rick and they were having a close conversation and I felt bad for being mad at her, and yet I was still mad at her. And I also had to thank her for a party even though I didn't want a party.

Or maybe I did want a party. It was confusing.

I didn't know how to have fun. I figured that out right then, in the middle of a living room full of people who generously came to my house and left me a stack of cards and presents. I didn't know how to have fun.

I made my way to Ellie and said, "Thank you!"

She smiled. "I thought you'd kill me the minute you heard *Surprise*."

"Nah. It's okay. It's really nice."

"You should celebrate graduating," she said. "It's a big deal."

"I guess."

She shook her head in semidisappointment. "It's a ticket out, Glory." Even Rick nodded at this. "It's, like, a ticket to the next thing in your future. Right?"

"Yeah. Of course," I said.

"No pressure, though," Ellie said. "Don't let all these college-bound dorks make you feel bad for what you want to do."

That made me laugh.

"Well, thanks," I said.

"Thank your aunt," Ellie said. "She paid for it."

I made my way to Aunt Amy, who was talking to Ed Heffner and Dad. She smiled as if I was her own daughter or something. Maybe she was happy to finally bring me some sort of normalcy.

They were really talking—I don't know about what—but I managed a quick hug and she knew what it was for.

Someone had stacked board games in random places. The yearbook club was already setting up Star Wars Trivial Pursuit on the back patio. No one seemed disappointed that there was no beer. Someone had music playing from their phone. Two citronella candles burned in the middle of the tables. I stood there and watched them all having fun. At my house. It was weird.

"If I had a choice, I'd take a year off before college too," Stacy Cullen said. Randomly. Blurted. From behind me. "It's cool that your dad's letting you do it."

"He's cool, all right."

"You were really surprised, weren't you?" she asked. "I mean, this party."

"Still am," I said, watching the Trivial Pursuit game.

"Not many people can be surprised by a graduation party, you know?"

"I'm weird. What can I say?"

"You're not weird," she said. "I bet half the graduating class wishes they were as cool as you."

I laughed. "I don't think I've ever been cool in my life."

"Bullshit. Seriously."

I was supposed to say something then, but instead I just thought *Am I really cool?* over and over again. Then Stacy's boyfriend asked her if she wanted to play LIFE and they disappeared back inside.

"Glory, where's your yearbook?" one of the yearbook kids asked.

"I don't know. Probably in my room."

"I never got to sign it," he said.

"That's okay," I said. "Don't worry about it."

"Hey, I didn't sign it either," someone said.

"Me neither," another yearbook clubber said.

Dad turned on some Led Zeppelin pretty loud from inside and I was going to tell him to turn it down, but then I figured if it was loud, I wouldn't have to talk as much.

"Get it!" someone else said, presumably about my yearbook. I didn't get it.

Instead, I went into the kitchen, where Aunt Amy had arranged some snacks—some for the commune people from the Whole Foods store and some for everyone else. There were cheese curls.

And root beer.

So I opened a root beer and picked up the entire bowl of cheese curls and carried it with me. Maybe if I had my hands full, no one would ask me for my yearbook again.

I met Ellie on her way to the kitchen as I was coming out.

"I see you found the fluorescent orange snacks."

"So all the talk about Markus Glenn coming to your party tonight was bullshit?"

"He was supposed to come *here*, actually," she said, which made me wonder if she knew me at all. "But I told my mom about him and she said he wasn't allowed anywhere near me."

"And Rick is?" I asked.

"Rick is."

"Okay, then," I said. "Just tell him to keep his Jupiterians off my toilet seat."

Ellie's dad talked to me for a while out in the yard, which was lit by a few citronella torches. He sat down next to me on a bench as I cleared the entire bowl of cheese curls and I stared into the sky and prayed—or whatever it meant to ask the sky for something—that the curse of the petrified bat would go away. I didn't want to know anybody else's future. I didn't care about anyone's past. I just wanted to go back to the present. Here. Now. This party where people thought I was cool.

Ellie's dad said, "We were all close once, you know."

"I know."

He sighed. "I regret what happened."

"I bet," I said. I said it like I knew what had happened because I wanted him to know that I knew what had happened. "So, did you talk to my dad? You guys make up or whatever?"

"Not quite."

"Oh."

"Sometimes too much time passes. It's been a long time. I regret what happened."

"You already said that."

"Yes. I guess I did."

"I regret a lot of things, too," I said.

"You're too young for that. You're only seventeen. Things happen for a reason, even shitty things. Does that make sense?"

"Yeah. That makes sense."

He caught my eye and I got a transmission from him against my will. Transmission from Ed Heffner: *One day Ellie will be standing in the commune's field alone. She will be crying. She will be surrounded by ducks that walk upright. She will step into a car and will never come back.*

I didn't want to see that.

I told myself Ellie was right. The transmissions were all bullshit. None of this could be right. Ellie wouldn't leave and Rick wasn't the grandfather of the man in the red pickup truck . . . who would eventually harm my family.

It was all bullshit. Fertilizer. Poppycock. I went inside.

Someone playing LIFE was pretending to cry because she had too many little plastic children to fit into her car. Someone else was rocking out with Dad to "Black Dog." I felt like something was missing, so I went to Dad's room and retrieved a picture of Darla and put it on the mantelpiece so she could smile at all of us instead of smiling at Dad's empty room.

At some point, the game of LIFE ended and after they all got to Millionaire Acres and counted their money, a winner was declared. At some point, someone had set up Jenga on the table that Dad usually used for his feet when he was working on the couch.

Then Aunt Amy made Dad turn down the music and yelled, "It's time for cake!" As she cut it and divvied it up, she told me to open presents.

"I'll wait," I said. "Isn't that what most people do?"

"Don't forget to send thank-yous," she said, still cutting perfect squares.

Don't forget to send thank-yous. What a concept. I hadn't even opened the presents yet, but I already had this social responsibility based on Aunt Amy's rules of gift-receiving. As if every gift giver is doing it for the thank-you note to come.

I looked at the stack of cards and looked around the room.

Everyone was having a good time. People were commenting that the cake was especially moist.

Jasmine didn't eat any cake. I took a plate of cake and a fork and I walked over to her and said hello.

She smiled a pained smile—the same pained smile I had and Dad had and Ed Heffner had. I looked over at Darla-on-the-mantel. She did not have a pained smile. She was no longer in pain.

I don't know what Jasmine and I talked about. We stood there for about two minutes, her making chitchat and me eating and nodding and realizing that Jasmine didn't know what was going to happen.

She did stupid things. Yes.

She did mean things, sure, but I was still wondering if Dad suffered some form of flattery from what happened and if that was the secret I would never know.

What I did know was that she wasn't to blame.

She just did what she did.

Then she did what she was told to do. She stayed away from our family and our house, and even Darla's funeral.

And now she was here.

Making chitchat. Not eating cake. Not touching a wall, a chair. Just there. Uncomfortable. I bet she couldn't wait to walk back across the road and escape all those haunting pictures.

She said, "Do you want more cake?"

I said, "Yes." And I walked toward the cake and the pile of pre-thank-you cards.

"Did you get it?" one of the yearbook kids asked me.

"What?"

"Your yearbook."

"No."

"Go get it," Matt said. "I want to sign it."

I saw Jasmine walk out the front door and I saw Ed Heffner watch her. He was talking to Dad, who had switched the music to some down-tempo live Grateful Dead.

I went to my bedroom and got my signature-free yearbook. After the party was over, it would be the one gift I got that didn't require a thank-you card.

People passed it around and signed things in it. Some of them took forever. Stacy Cullen had it for ten whole minutes. One of the yearbook clubbers drew a cartoon starring me and my camera. And then, Ellie. She spent a long time writing on the inside cover, which everyone had saved for her on account of her being my best friend . . . even if I'd forgotten that she was my best friend.

By this time, the Star Wars Trivial Pursuit game was over and the reigning champion was promised ten dollars apiece by the losers. As people signed my book, they left and hugged each other and me and said thank you and I gave some of them extra cake because I didn't plan on sending thank-you notes.

Ellie and Rick left last, along with Stacy Cullen and her boyfriend. Stacy whispered in my ear that she'd lied to her mom and told her she was sleeping over at my house, and asked if I would cover for her. I said yes. I said, "Be safe."

Ellie handed me my yearbook on her way out the door and said she'd see me tomorrow.

I closed the door behind them all and went out to the patio to read through the things people said. They all started in the same way: *To a cool girl I met in... To a mysterious girl I met when... To a fun girl I met when... To a talented photographer and friend... To a great friend I met in... To a nice kid who turned out to be a nicer adult...*

One of the entries talked about how I'd seen the world differently than others. One entry talked about how my life had started bumpy but it meant that I was heading to greatness. So many predictions.

I had a book full of my own predictions. *The History of the Future.* But I preferred this book to my own. I preferred these predictions. I preferred being a cool/mysterious/fun/talented/nice girl rather than the girl who would one day be known only for a prediction of suffering.

Layers

Aunt Amy was cleaning up in the kitchen and I went downstairs to help her. She talked to Dad as if they'd been friends for a lifetime, and I guess they had been. I never saw it that way before—how adults have lives on top of lives on top of lives. Layers. Maybe that was why Ed Heffner told me I shouldn't have regrets now. Maybe there were too many regrets to come. Or maybe now was the time to stop having them so there weren't too many later. Or something.

"You looked like you had a good time," Aunt Amy said.

"It was great. Thank you so much." I said this and realized I wanted to send at least one thank-you note . . . to her.

"How about we sit and open those cards now?" She dried her hands on a tea towel and cracked open one of Dad's beers. He cracked one open too, and then went out to the patio to blow out the citronella candles and tidy up. I grabbed another root beer.

Nearly every card had a gift card in it. Some were bookstore gift cards. Some were clothing store gift cards. Online store gift cards. Restaurant gift cards. Home furnishing gift cards.

Aunt Amy counted the cash value. I'm not sure why. Maybe that's what normal people do.

"Three hundred and seventy-five dollars," she said. "That'll buy a heck of a lot of books." She handed me an unopened envelope. "From me and my family," she said, as if I wasn't aware of her husband and fragile-necked children.

The card was pink and it had a cartoon of a graduate on the front—a female graduate with high heels on. And jewelry. Lots of jewelry.

The inside was blank, and Aunt Amy had written in it. I could only read what she wrote when I moved the hundred-dollar check out of the way.

My sister was the only sibling I had. When I lost her, I felt like I lost everything. But then, there was you.

I wanted to come around more and see you but my own family grew. Your dad would keep me updated as you went from little girl to big girl to teenager, and all the while, I prayed that you would grow into the type of woman Darla was.

You have.

You are creative, resourceful, intelligent, strong, funny and beautiful.

I don't want to make you sad on such a special day, but I want you to know how proud Darla is of you today.

*She loved you so much and I can't imagine how much
you must miss her.*

*Keep in touch, Glory. Let me know if you need any-
thing. Let me know if you want to talk. Maybe I can fill
a tiny piece of the hole she left, the way you fill a piece of
the hole she left in me.*

I love you. Congratulations.

Dad came in then, which was probably bad timing. If I
could have, I would have sat and talked to Aunt Amy about my
mother for the rest of the night. Darla's darkroom didn't have
the answers. *Why People Take Pictures* didn't have the answers.
Dad didn't really have the answers. No one would have all the
answers except Darla. That's how suicide goes. No one has all
the answers except the person you can't ask anymore.

But Aunt Amy would be able to talk about so much
because she lost a sister to suicide and that couldn't have been
easy either. But now Dad was there, jovial and a little tipsy and
asking if we wanted to play Scrabble.

"Or poker if you want. Amy was always a shark at poker."
I had to dry my eyes quietly on my sleeve and Amy did, too.
On her sleeve, not mine. Dad noticed. "Or...I can go back to
the porch and mind my own business if you want."

"No," Aunt Amy said. "It's fine. Stay here. I'd love to kick
your ass in poker, Roy, but only if we play for real money."

"You two finish talking and come out when you're ready.
I've been practicing, Amy. Don't be too cocky." He walked out
of the room.

Aunt Amy called after him, "Playing a computer isn't real practice, you know!"

Then we looked at each other.

Transmission from Aunt Amy: *Her grandson will run a safe house for orphans and will find them new homes, all under the radar of the new laws and New American Army. The safe house looks very familiar. It will be Ellie's barn. The one across the road.*

"I want to talk about a lot of things," I said. "But not tonight."

"Let's make time this summer. I have time."

I had beginner's luck and beat Dad and Aunt Amy on my first hand of poker. Apparently I had a full house, which doesn't look like much, but it beat Dad's pair of queens and Aunt Amy's three of a kind.

After that, Amy wiped the floor with us and Dad had to pay her sixty bucks.

When she left, I went upstairs and piled my gift cards and graduation cards on my dresser and I changed into my pajamas. I felt like a snack, so I went back downstairs.

Dad motioned for me to sit down.

"About that law," he said. "I looked it up."

I nodded.

"I think your mom would want me to get it back."

I nodded again, but my insides twisted because now it all seemed wrong. Now everything was different. Maybe because of the party. Maybe because of the bat. Maybe because of graduating from high school. Maybe because—just because.

"I could die anytime and I wouldn't want to leave you with that mess. It wouldn't be fair."

"Nah. You won't die until you're old," I said. "Trust me."

He gave me a look. "I guess I should have talked to you about everything before this week. Sorry about that."

"Don't be sorry," I said. "The details were...awkward. I get it."

I had an urge to talk him out of taking the land back, but I knew he was right. We did have to get it back. I knew Darla had given it as a gift, but it was always going to be temporary. You can't have a free place to stay for nineteen years and not think the end is coming.

It's a little like being a kid and graduating high school and moving on.

Glory O'Brien's History of the Future

Nedrick's former followers will go to the governor's mansion in the last state under Nedrick's power and they will burn it to the ground. (Upon the mansion's evacuation, they will discover that the governor still employs several women, against his own law.) Nedrick the Sanctimonious will still blame exiles and outcasts, but the revolt will come from within.

The people will be so angry. So angry.

The people will wonder how they ended up slaves when only years before they were normal Americans eating microwave popcorn and waxing leased cars.

The exiles, the Sniper, and her husband will be far from the governor's mansion. They will be waiting for the final battle. From underground, they will hear the armies move into place. They will hear how outnumbered Nedrick is. They will know he is there. They will feel him.

Early on a Tuesday morning, they will hear the ground above them rumble and creak. They will hear it fill with soldier after soldier. They will empty the tunnels and will call for full retreat. The Sniper will tell the exiles where to go. She will send them far from the coming explosions. Far from harm.

She will clean her rifle.

He will press the button.

And the final chapter will begin with a kapow.

People still do that

It was Friday and Peter looked genuinely happy to see me. I didn't want to jump to conclusions, but I think he enjoyed my company. I felt that every time I saw him in June would increase my chances of being the soul mate he finds in the mall during June 2014.

"By yourself today?"

"Yeah," I said.

He pointed to my camera. I'd found Darla's old camera strap and I'd attached it this morning before I left. Dad had approved. He said it made him happy it was getting used again.

She'd hand-embroidered it with butterflies.

"You taking pictures?" Peter asked.

"It's part of my project," I said.

He smiled at a passerby. Then he marked an *X* on his clipboard. The guy walked past him reading something on his smartphone and never even looked up.

"You should have a separate category for those," I said. "It's different than just ignoring you, isn't it?"

"They know I'm there. They can probably feel me smiling. They just don't look up."

"You'd think, after that video of the woman falling into the fountain, people wouldn't do that in this mall."

"People need their information, man. They have to have it right there, right then, twenty-four-seven."

"True," I said, thinking of Dad and how often he checked his e-mail account even though he didn't have any friends and usually, it was just spam trying to sell him penis pills, Canadian pharmaceuticals, online dating or mythical free lobster.

"So what are you taking pictures of?" he asked.

"I don't know," I said. "When I see something, I take the picture. Until then, I have no idea."

"Take one of me smiling at people, will you? It would add to the project. Might get me extra credit," he said.

I nodded to the approaching people and I backed away and to the left so I could get the backs of the mall patrons' heads and the front of Peter's face as he smiled with his clipboard in hand. I snapped a few shots of him looking at them and then a few shots of him marking it down on his clipboard.

When three women approached, I moved to a different angle and got pictures of their interactions, too. One of those women smiled back. She let her friends walk on and asked Peter what he was selling. I wasn't very far away, so I heard their conversation.

"If you were selling kisses, I'd buy one," she said.

"I'm not selling anything," he said.

"Can I give you my number?" she asked.

Peter looked embarrassed. But he took her number and then he watched her walk away. She swung her hips and swooshed her platinum hair and she even stopped when she got to her friends and they all turned around and giggled.

It pained me to think she might be the one in Peter's transmission. She didn't scream *soul mate*, but what did I know? I was still a virgin who liked to drown herself in seersucker dresses. I was still trying to be Darla, even though I knew I wasn't Darla, embroidered butterflies and all.

"Did you get any good shots?" he asked.

Transmission from Peter: *He will climb to a tree house to rescue a baby from the fire. He will climb so fast, they will joke afterward about how he might be part monkey. His hair will be white. He will be old when this happens. When he rescues the baby, he will give it back to its mother and they will make their way through the forest to the tunnels.*

"Glory?" he asked.

"Yeah. I got some good ones. Of the dude who totally ignored you and of the woman giving you her number."

He looked embarrassed again. "Cool," he said. "Can you send them to me when you upload them?"

I held the camera up and waved it a little. "It's real film. I have to develop it first."

"Oh," he said. "I didn't know people still did that."

"People still do that," I said.

He got up and smiled at a person walking by, then marked the *X* on his clipboard. I eyed the increasing mall traffic.

"I'll see you for lunch?" I asked.

"You bet," he said.

I thought about how he eats sweet-and-sour chicken. I thought about how maybe that woman who gave him her number was a perfect banal match. They could be the sweet-and-sour chicken eaters in the world and I could be on the kung pao beef hot-and-spicy eater team. My team would probably be better at Ping-Pong and have better immune systems. Their team would most likely have better dress sense and larger closets.

Oh well.

I felt self-conscious with my camera. People at the mall stared at me. They seemed to cringe at the idea of a person taking pictures of them. I found this odd when everyone has a built-in camera on their phone now. Why be freaked out by my old-fashioned camera when someone could be taking your picture all the time without you knowing?

I limited my pictures to nonhuman things. Signs. Empty benches. Fountains. Doors. Elevator buttons.

"Hey! It's you again," USS *Pledge* guy said to me just as I was walking out of the elevator. "My calzone friend!"

I smiled and gave him a wave. "I've been looking for you!"

"What you got there? Is that a real camera?"

"A Canon AE1," I said. "Vintage 1980. Nothing special."

"I used to use a Leica. I loved those damn things. Something about them."

"My mom has two of them in the attic." I didn't tell him about the Leica she'd given me when I was four. I don't know why.

"Oh!" he said, so excited to be talking about Leicas. "You should dig them out and try 'em. They're something else."

I nodded and wasn't sure what to say.

"You coming up for calzone today?" he asked.

"Sure," I said. "Are you meeting your friends or can we eat together?"

"Are you asking me on a date?" he said. He winked as he said it.

"Sure," I said. "Why not?"

And so we pushed the elevator button for the second floor once he wheeled himself in.

The Sniper

"Do you want me to push you?" I asked as the elevator pulled us toward the second floor.

"I've been wheeling myself around since 1951 and I don't plan on stopping today," he said.

We stood (he sat) in line for our calzones and I ordered a spinach and cheese and he ordered a plain but asked the manager to put hot peppers in it for him.

Here was my teammate on the hot-and-spicy team. I might have been wrong about the Ping-Pong.

I moved a chair out of the way so he could wheel up to the table and we opened our calzone boxes and let them cool off. He asked me to grab a few more napkins and I did.

"How come you're here all the time?" he asked.

"I'm doing a project," I said, and motioned toward the camera.

"In the summer? A school project?"

"Nah. It's for me. I guess I made it up."

"That's pretty smart," he said. "Keeping yourself busy until school starts again. What are you? Fifteen?"

"Seventeen. I just graduated."

"The older I get, the younger you all look," he said. "Yesterday I swear I saw a nine-year-old driving a tractor-trailer."

I laughed.

"Can I ask you about your hat?" I asked. "I know one of the USS *Pledge* boats sank in Korea. Was that your boat?"

"You're putting me on," he said.

"What?"

"No one your age cares about Korea."

I shook my head and finished chewing my calzone. "It was a minesweeper, right? Sunk in 1950?"

He let out a laugh like I'd just told the funniest joke he'd ever heard. I thought this meant I'd said something stupid, so I quickly corrected myself. "Oh. Maybe you were on the one in Vietnam, then. The other USS *Pledge*?"

"No no. You got it right. I was sunk in Korea. Dragged out of the water and never felt my legs again," he said. He shook his head. "My son says no one your age gives a flying squirrel about old wars now. I bet my grandson doesn't know anything about anything."

"Huh," I said.

"He's been brought up in some kind of cult, anyway. Can't imagine they're allowed to do much thinking for themselves. What a joke," he said.

I stopped eating and looked at him. Transmission from USS *Pledge* guy: *His mother didn't want him to go to war. She thought it was wrong. She blamed him for his injury for the rest of her life.*

"A cult? That's interesting," I said. "I never knew anyone in a cult." I wasn't really following as he spoke. I thought the grandson he was talking about was some far-off grandson on the West Coast or something, and the cult was like those unicorn-loving people Dad's mother ran off with. But then I remembered who he was—who his grandson was.

"I think all they teach the kids out there is how to freeload off the government. Because..."

"That place is a cult?" I asked. I put my calzone down. "The place out by the lake? With all the RVs?"

"I used to call the cops and ask if I could at least get my grandson out. No luck."

"What's your grandson's name?" I asked again.

He lowered his eyebrows. "You're not one of them, are you?"

"No."

"His name is Richard. After me! Can you believe that?"

"I know him," I said. "I've met him a few times." He looked at me like this hurt him—me knowing Rick better than he did. "I'll say hi to him if you want."

"I wish you'd just smuggle him out," he said. He was joking now, smiling and eating his calzone. "Or maybe you can tell him about the *Pledge* and how I ended up in this chair. I don't think he knows, and I bet my idiot son never told him the truth, either."

"I'll do it next time I see him," I said. Then I picked up my camera. "I don't usually do this, but do you mind if I take a few pictures of you?"

He let me and I snapped a bunch of him at different exposures because I wanted to capture every age spot on his face and every wrinkle. He was a good-looking man for over eighty years old. I told him that.

"It's not nice to tease senior citizens," he said.

"I'm not teasing. I bet you were one handsome kid when you were my age."

"Tell you the truth, I had acne and I was awkward on my feet. Never good at sports or dancing. Always good at math."

I lowered the camera and looked at him, and I was hit with something I couldn't describe. It was a mix of panic attack and transmission.

What I saw made me light-headed. It made me dizzy. Made me nauseous.

Transmission from wheelchair-bound Richard USS *Pledge* guy:

I will be in the tunnel.

Glory O'Brien with stark white hair and wearing men's combat pants. I will be in the tunnel as it fills with smoke.

I will be with Peter, also white-haired and combat-geared, and a male child.

Behind us will stand about twenty exiles with masks on to block out the smoke. In front of us will stand Nedrick the Sanctimonious's red-pickup-truck-driving right-hand man. He will be holding a flamethrower. The boy? Will be his boy. He will have curly hair and psoriasis. He will have bare feet because his mother will have been forced to live in the trees for the last three years. He will recognize his father and plead with him not to burn us. His father will choose to burn us anyway because I will be the leader of the resistance, and I will be enemy number one.

The Sniper. Far more important than some bastard son.

"Are you okay?" someone asked me. It could have been anyone.

"Glory?" That was Peter.

Somebody caught me as I slumped out of my chair.

Richard USS *Pledge* said, "Give the poor girl some air."

I would live

The room spun. I saw myself in the tunnel. I saw the boy. I saw the flames. The smoke. I don't remember anything after that until I opened my eyes and I was sitting on the floor next to Peter, who was holding a Chinese takeout container.

Once I said I felt well enough, he helped move me back to my chair at the table where Richard the USS *Pledge* guy was still sitting. I explained that I got panic attacks sometimes and I apologized. I sat there not making eye contact with either of them. Richard had to go because he had an appointment at the eye doctor.

He reminded me, "Don't forget to tell little Richard I say hello if you see him. I miss that kid. Will you tell him that?"

I told him I'd tell him.

Peter ate chicken fried rice while I sat there and figured out my part in the history of the future.

It was all pretty simple. *I* was the family member who would be harmed in that tunnel. Not my child or grandchild. I will be an old woman and Peter will be an old man. And I will be the leader of the exiles.

I watched Peter eat his chicken fried rice with a plastic fork. We would be married one day. No hurry.

I looked around the mall. All those people would be dead one day, just like I would be. No hurry.

As I put Darla's camera back around my neck, I realized that I was no part Darla. I was not on my way to the oven, not on my way to the closed garage with the car keys and not in any way like Bill the headless man who blew his brains into rancid ceiling art.

I would live. *I would really live.*

I took a picture of Peter eating his lunch and smiled at him. This might have been a flirtatious smile. I know it wasn't the same kind of smile I'd given him a half hour before. This was more of a one-day-I'm-going-to-be-your-wife smile. I don't know why, but it made him look at me in a whole new way. We locked eyes.

But I didn't get a transmission.

Weird.

I looked right at him—stared right into his pupils.

Still nothing.

"What are you looking at?" he asked.

"Um. You?" I answered.

Still no transmission. I said I wanted dessert so I went to Señor Burrito and ordered fried ice cream. On my way, I made eye contact with three people. No transmissions. The old guy who's always working at Señor Burrito? No transmission. The lady on her lunch break from the hair salon? No transmission. I tried Peter again when I got back to the table. Still nothing.

I shared the fried ice cream with him and we didn't say much between bites.

The sky had answered my sky-prayer.

The bat was gone.

That's all

Peter smiled at people while I finished the fried ice cream myself.

"What do you think about cults?" I asked.

"I'm . . . uh . . . against them as a rule?"

I didn't say anything.

"Why?" he asked.

"I think Ellie lives in one. I mean, Richard—the guy I had lunch with—he thinks Ellie lives in one."

"Oh."

"I always saw cults as some sort of bigger thing—like, you know, Jim Jones or Jonestown or something," I said. I'd read all about Jim Jones in the eighth grade. He killed nearly a thousand people, but the media made us believe they all committed suicide. Jim Jones got the last laugh.

"Well, shit," Peter said. "Doesn't she live across the street? You'd know if it was like that, wouldn't you?"

"I don't know. Yeah. I guess I would."

When I said good-bye to Peter that day, I decided to treat him as if we'd know each other for a lifetime. He did too. He asked if I'd see him the next day. I told him I probably would, but if not, I'd call him. He smiled. I smiled. And then, on my way home, I really tried to fathom it. Jasmine Blue: cult leader. It didn't seem plausible.

If Jasmine Blue Heffner believed a microwave oven was an atomic bomb, then I wondered what she would think of HC-110 developer or worse yet, photographic fixer with its 97% hydroquinone. I bet she'd think a darkroom was a Nazi gas chamber and I was a willing victim, walking in as if it was a shower, all the while holding my mother's hand.

If Jasmine Blue gave naked pictures of herself to men, then how would she answer Darla's final question?

Why do people take pictures?

Or, in this case, why do people take naked pictures?

Is it to fasten that moment in time? The moment when your thighs are still consumerist-perfect and your hair is consumerist-styled right and your body is just like all the bodies in the consumerist magazines people buy? Anyone who tried to convince me that Jasmine wasn't a gorging consumerist on the inside from today onward wouldn't succeed.

The woman was fat with consumerism.

And nobody in that commune knew it.

Richard of the USS *Pledge* was right—maybe the commune was a cult in a way. Jasmine controlled when the kids would graduate. She controlled when people did anything. Star parties. Day trips. Local protests. But I didn't see her going all doomsday like Jim Jones at Jonestown. I didn't see her killing anyone. I didn't see her using mind control or making anyone miserable.

Jasmine needed to be liked. That's all. And who doesn't need to be liked, right?

Glory O'Brien's History of the Future

The explosion at the battlefield will scatter parts of Nedrick's New American Army in all directions. Arms. Legs. Heads. Hands. Ears. The tunnels will rumble. The Sniper will run quickly to the safer tunnels, her husband close behind her, until they find a boy. The boy will beg them to stop. The boy will say there is too much smoke. He will say they are trapped. He is familiar to me. He will have come from a safe house that looks like Ellie's barn.

They will hear footsteps from behind. There will be a flamethrower and a man. The head of Ferret Company who has hunted them for over a year. A man who drives a red pickup truck.

"Why don't you come with us?" the Sniper will say.

The man will consider this. He will look at the boy. Something will change in him when he sees the boy. Something will soften.

"It's over," he'll say. "I've found you."

The boy will think the man is talking about him and will run toward him. The man will fire his flamethrower at the three of them: the Sniper, her husband and the boy.

But it will not be over. Nothing is ever over until there is no breath left. And when he leaves them there, scorched and bloody, they will be breathing.

I can't see ... anything

Ellie came over when she saw me on the porch in the rocking chair. I'd eaten dinner with Dad and stared at him a lot, trying to see a transmission, but I couldn't see a thing.

She sat on the step and leaned against the railing.

"The ... *thing* ... it's gone. I can't see ... anything," she said.

"I know," I said. "Me too."

"What are you doing tonight?" she asked.

"Nothing," I lied. I'd planned on printing some negatives.

"We should do something to celebrate the bat being gone, don't you think?"

"I guess we should," I said.

I went inside and told Dad I'd be home later.

This time there was no jar full of dust. Just beer. Ellie offered me one.

"No thanks," I said.

"It's cold this time," Ellie said. "I got it straight from my dad's fridge."

I shook my head again and she cracked open her beer.

She didn't want to talk about the transmissions. She didn't want to talk about the war, *my war*, she called it, because I'm pretty sure she didn't really think it was coming. She didn't want to talk about Rick because she knew I already knew too much about Rick.

I grew awkwardly silent.

Without Max Black, I had nothing in common with her anymore.

So I watched the sky turn its sunset colors. There weren't many. Some sunsets are boring. This one was.

"I wrote the history of the future," I said.

"What?"

"I wrote the history of the future."

"Like Nostradamus. He did that, right?" she said.

"Kinda," I said.

"Maybe one day you'll be famous," she said.

"I don't want to be famous. I kinda hope what I saw never happens."

"Yeah," she said.

Before it got dark, she'd had two beers, we'd talked about pretty much every type of small talk there was—memories of our childhood, a few bad jokes—and when Ellie noticed that I hadn't said anything for a while, she sighed—as if reality was a hassle—and said, "So did you ever find your wheelchair guy? Did he help you write this paper or what?"

"It's not a paper. It's a book," I said. "And yeah. We had lunch together today. With Peter."

"Peter," she said. "Good."

"The weirdest thing is that the old guy's related to Rick. It's his grandfather. Weird, huh?"

"I can't wait to get the fuck out of there," Ellie said, clearly not hearing a word I said. "Can I use your cell phone to call Markus Glenn?"

Oh well.

I gave her my phone, and once she'd made the date, I said good night and walked home. It wasn't my job to save Ellie.

So the only person left for me to deal with was Dad. Roy O'Brien—whose ancestors ate giant stag over a fire—chronic microwaver, occasional Jazzy driver and painting avoider.

It wasn't my job to save him. But I wanted to try. I wanted him to see *Why People Take Pictures*. I wanted to tell him about *The History of the Future*, too. Then maybe he'd stop wasting so much time on the couch.

Darla Darla Darla

Before I went downstairs in the morning, I grabbed *The History of the Future*. I was scared about this part the most. Maybe if I told Dad what I'd seen, he'd think I was losing it like Darla had. I'd never shared my fear of becoming Darla with him, either, so I didn't know if he was hiding that same fear from me, too.

But before I could make it down to the living room, Dad called out, "Cupcake? Can you come here?"

He had two folders on the couch next to him and papers around those. Laptop in place, he read me part of Pennsylvania's squatters' rights law.

"So that makes it sound like we have twenty-one years, right? Even if they have a claim in?"

"That's what it sounds like to me," I said. "You could always call a lawyer."

"Well, I kinda did. Yesterday."

"Oh."

"We have options," he said. "And I talked to a guy I know at the township office, too."

"Did Jasmine put a claim in for the land?"

"She wouldn't do that," he said.

"Never know."

"It won't matter anyhow," he said, handing me one of the papers. "I'm gonna give her this later. I'm gonna send one in the mail first to be official, then I'm going to walk this copy over."

"Only fair," I said, while reading the letter. It was the same as the one I'd written but instead of my signature, it was his—minus the love. Short and sweet. Attached to it was a cover letter that explained zoning laws and how the township had contacted him about a list of things. Too many RVs. Too many people living in a noncompliant structure (the barn). And apparently, no one on the commune had paid per capita taxes except for Ed, who'd been paying just for himself and Jasmine. The letter was nice. Almost apologetic.

"Thanks for making me do this," he said. "I've been in the same hole for a long time and I never wanted to step out." He looked at the letter again when I handed it back to him. "I mean, how will they ever know what the real world is like if I give them a free place to stay for the rest of their lives?"

I looked at him then. "Are you trying to tell me something?"

We laughed.

"I still think she'll freak out," he said. "But my hands are tied now. I have to get them off the property."

I said, "So, can we talk about painting now?"

"Not really."

"Too late."

He looked at me over his computer glasses.

"I have an assignment for you. Could be one single piece, could be a whole series," I said. "But I think it will be good."

"Okay," he said.

I took a deep breath. "Ovens." I drew one with my hands—boxy, rectangular. I pulled the imaginary door open. "I think you should paint ovens."

"Shit."

"Think about it. A summer project. Summer is only starting now. You quit that lame job and you can paint and I'll print in the darkroom and then I'll figure out what I'm really going to do with my life now that everything has changed."

"Everything has changed, huh?"

I couldn't tell him about the future even though I was holding *The History of the Future* in my hands. "Trust me. Everything has changed."

————

I put both sketchbooks back in the darkroom for another day. And then I went to the bank. I won't tell you what I went to the bank for because you would think I was nuts. But what about me wasn't already nuts?

I went to the bank. I walked inside and I did something.

The thing I did made me smile.

When I got home and back into the darkroom, I looked at Darla's tooth, still lying on the counter where I'd left it. I decided to tack it back on the ceiling along with its message. *Not living your life is just like killing yourself, only it takes longer.*

It would be my mistletoe again—and every time I walked under it, it would give me good luck until I was strong enough to be the leader of the resistance.

Dad went to the post office while I printed four pictures.

One of Richard the USS *Pledge* guy. It was a good shot. He was grinning a bit and had a look in his eye like he was proud to know me—a girl who knew about his war.

The next image I printed was of the elevator button. It said OPEN DOORS.

The third one was of Peter looking at me in the food court. His face held a genuine smile—as if maybe one day we'd be together until our hair turned white. As if maybe something about me was loveable. Nothing about a tipi. Nothing about boobs. Peter looked as if he liked my brain. If that's possible to capture in a picture, then I captured it.

Then I printed the picture of me in the bat glasses. It was so badass. I taped it into *The History of the Future* and wrote: *Glory O'Brien, Sniper. Mad at the World.*

I looked at our sketchbooks—Darla's and mine—sitting side by side, and I read the titles. *Why People Take Pictures* and *The History of the Future.* That's what pictures are. They are the history of the future. They will outlive us and they will exist to show us that even if it's gone, even if it's never going to tuck you in at night or sing you a lullaby, it is still there, in silver halide and paper. It is there because you can look at it and remember. It is powerful because once it's there, it changes as you change.

"I'm going over!" Dad yelled down the steps.

"Wait up!" I answered. My prints were all in the washer, so I turned on the big light and went upstairs.

He looked nervous.

"Don't be nervous," I said. "Your hands are tied, remember?"

He didn't answer me and he started across the road and toward Jasmine's house. I sat on the rocking chair on the front porch and watched him.

Ed Heffner came to the door first and gave Dad one of those half-hug handshakes and I think he invited Dad in, but Dad stayed on the rickety old porch and eventually Jasmine Blue came out.

Dad said some stuff. That's why I stayed on the porch. I wanted him to be able to say whatever he wanted to say. Jasmine said some stuff. Ed tried to say some stuff but then Jasmine held her hand up to make him be quiet. Ed looked at his feet for a minute while Dad and Jasmine exchanged more words.

Then Dad handed her the letter, nodded a good-bye to Ed and walked down the steps and back toward me.

As soon as Dad got to the road, Jasmine started toward him. She wasn't saying anything, but she was fast-walking, the ripped envelope and the unfolded letter in her hand. Her hippie dress got caught between her hurried legs. By the time he crossed the road and landed on the front porch next to me, she was waiting for a car to pass and looking right at us.

"You can't do this!" she said.

"I have no choice," he said.

"It's rightfully ours!" she said as she crossed the road.

"Show me the receipt from the last time you paid taxes on it," he said.

"We don't believe in taxes," she said. "And you know it."

"Must be nice."

She sighed and growled under her breath. "Why are you doing this, Roy? Can't you just let the whole thing go?"

"What whole thing?"

"Darla."

And there it was. Spoken aloud. By Jasmine Blue Heffner. *Darla.*

Darla.

Darla.

Darla.

"She was my wife," Dad said. "Exactly why would I let her go? This is her house. Glory is her daughter." He knocked on the rocking chair arm. *"This was her fucking rocking chair. And that"*—he pointed to Jasmine's commune—*"is her land."*

"And you're going to steal it from us," she said.

He said, "I can't steal something that's already mine. Anyway, did you read the letter? It's not me. It's the township, too. Can't you just be happy you got to live the dream for as long as you did?"

"You always were a fat, greedy asshole."

I think Dad was as shocked by this reaction as I was.

Although maybe we weren't. Maybe we both knew that Jasmine was a self-centered jerk who thought lawyers and townships and tax collectors were all beneath her. Along with us.

"Sure I was," he said. "That's why you sent me all those pretty pictures, right? Because I was a fat, greedy asshole?"

She said, "You'll hear from my lawyer."

And Dad answered, "If you want to do it the hard way, I'll go copy the paperwork from when you bought it from us. Except that doesn't exist. Bummer."

I laughed a little at that. More like a giggle.

She stood there and stared.

She looked at me. "You're as fucked up as your mother was."

I smiled. "Thank you."

———

During dinner, I could tell Dad was feeling bad. I said, "I can't believe she was so mean about it."

"I hope you didn't take that thing she said about Mom too personally. Jasmine is a self-centered jerk and she has always been a self-centered jerk."

I wanted to say something about the apple not falling far from the tree, but I didn't. Instead I just ate and thought about Ellie and what I'd seen in that last transmission from Ed Heffner.

Ellie and the ducks.

Ellie getting into a car.

Ellie gone. Forever.

I lost my appetite.

Like, today

The next day, Ellie came over at noon and told me they were moving.

"Like, today," she said. "They've been packing all night. They won't tell me why, but Rick told me it was because your dad took the land back."

"The township wrote us letters, I think. His hands were tied."

"So it *was* him?"

"More like the township," I said again. "Where are you going? Is it far?"

"I don't know."

"You don't know?"

"Another commune, I think. We're taking everything," she said. "But not the chickens." At this, she started to cry.

I went over and gave her a hug and she got snot all over my

ear and I didn't care. A week ago, she was treating her crabs in my barn. A week ago, we drank a bat and saw God. A week ago, we *were* God. Now we were mortal—swayed by the decisions our parents made.

"Will you take care of my birds for me?" she asked. "I have enough feed for a few months. Maybe you can sell the ducks back to where I got them. The chickens are good for fresh eggs." Ellie babbled some more things about chickens and ducks. I didn't hear all of what she said because I was trying to block out a feeling of deep guilt.

"Sure," I said. "Of course I'll take care of them."

"I told my parents I wanted to stay. I can't wait to get away from them all."

Dad, who must have overheard all of this from the kitchen, came in and said, "Why don't the two of you go for a drive?"

"A drive?" I asked. I was finally going to be free of Ellie, and now Dad wanted me to go for a *drive?*

Dad shrugged. "Maybe Ellie and you need a night to go and have fun somewhere. How about the shore? Your mothers used to love going to the beach together."

"The shore?" Ellie asked. "We're moving. I told you."

He nodded. "You've got choices, right?"

Ellie and I looked at each other.

"I don't know," she said.

"Want to try?"

Fifteen minutes later, we were driving down the highway. I felt free. Free of school. Free of regret. Free of Darla. Even free of Ellie, even though she was in my car. I looked at her, worried and nervous in the passenger's seat, and saw that she was not free of anything—especially Jasmine Blue.

"Are you sure you want to do this?" I asked.

"Where will we go?"

"Anywhere we want. How about the beach, like my dad suggested? It's only three hours away. Maybe we could just touch the ocean with our toes and come back. Just for fun," I said.

"The beach sounds nice," she said.

It did. It really did.

"Will you tell Markus Glenn what happened?" she asked. "When you see him? Tell him we moved away?" She started to cry then.

"Sure."

"Don't tell him I cried, though. He'll just think I'm an emotional girl."

"So? What's wrong with being an emotional girl?"

"Guys hate that."

"Who said?"

"Um. All guys."

I laughed. "What do they know?"

"I guess."

"Anyway, who cares what guys like? They don't do stuff because of what we like, right?"

"Sure," she said.

We stopped for a pee break an hour later at the New Jersey border rest stop. When I came out of the bathroom, I found Ellie standing there looking . . . sad? Lost?

We walked back to the car and it was clear that something was wrong.

"What if I never see them again?" she asked.

"I don't know."

"What if they just move and leave me behind?"

"You always told me you'd get out as soon as you could." I didn't want to make her feel bad. But I didn't want her to forget all the times she said she wanted out of there. "But I don't think they'd just leave you behind, Ellie."

"I know. But it's—uh..."

"You want me to turn around?"

"Yeah," she said, and started to cry again.

After a few minutes of her crying I said, "You can leave whenever you want. And you will, right? We saw it."

She just shook her head yes and kept crying into a now-soggy tissue.

"You're going to have a nice life. Kids. Two grandsons, remember?"

I took the next exit and turned around and went back west. I didn't mind. I had plenty of stuff to do at home—like buying an oven and printing pictures and getting on with my life because I was not Darla.

"Can I use your phone?" she asked.

She called her house and when Jasmine finally answered on the third try, she hadn't even noticed Ellie was gone with all the moving commotion at the commune. Most of the stuff was already en route.

"I'll be home in about...an hour?" Ellie said.

I didn't hear what Jasmine said, but it made Ellie say these things, in order.

"I'm an hour away. I can't be there in ten minutes."

"I can't tell you."

"Yes. I'm with Markus."

"No. Of course not."

"An hour."

"Fine. I'll wait for Dad, then."

She hung up.

"I guess today is our last day," she said. "It's been nice being your best friend."

"Same here," I said.

"Sorry for all the weird bullshit I must have pushed on you."

"Nah."

"Seriously. I told you your microwave was an atomic bomb."

"Well, it kinda is."

"Glory, your microwave oven is not an atomic bomb."

"Okay. Apology accepted."

"It's messed up," she said. "All of it."

"Yep."

I didn't know what she meant. I didn't know what she thought was messed up. What's messed up when you drink a bat? What's messed up when you see the history of the future? What's messed up when your best friend is an accidental semi–cult member? A dead mother? A book?

The bat had a message. It was dead. It had a message from the other side. It was: *Free yourself. Have the courage.* Whatever it meant to each one of us, it meant *something*.

Oh well

We got home in less than two hours and the commune was empty. The RVs were gone. The barn doors were open, airing out fifteen years' worth of semisanitary living conditions.

The only things left were the chickens and the ducks. Ellie went to spend time with them after she found her bedroom in the house empty.

Dad told me that Jasmine had come over and demanded to search the house for Ellie.

He told me that when Jasmine was rummaging around upstairs, he went to the darkroom and got *Why People Take Pictures* and opened the book to her old pictures "from the nineties" and left it on the dining room table so she could see it on her way out.

"You knew about *Why People Take Pictures?*" I asked.

He nodded.

He said Jasmine turned white when she saw the pictures. Ed was waiting on the front porch, so she couldn't say anything. She couldn't do anything. All she could do was wonder what we'd do with them now. Here was what we'd do with them now: nothing.

Oh well.

I had mixed feelings about the whole thing. I was glad Jasmine was gone. I was glad we had the land back. I was glad we could keep Ellie's chickens and ducks. Or, our chickens and ducks. Or whoever's birds they were now.

But I was sad about losing Ellie. After years of wanting to lose Ellie, I was sad about it. This was not an *oh well*. It was something, but it wasn't an *oh well*.

I went upstairs to change into shorts. Summer was coming—quickly.

When I came back downstairs, I found Dad on the front porch watching Ellie. She was hugging her ducks. One by one, picking the runner ducks up and hugging them.

I ran across the road and hugged her.

"You're going to be okay," I said.

"I'm never going to be okay," she said.

I pulled out the cashier's check from my pocket and handed it to her. It was folded in two. She opened it.

"Ten thousand dollars?"

"Don't tell anyone. Not anyone."

"Where did you *get* this?" she said. "I can't take it."

"You have to take it. It's a gift," I said. "It doesn't matter where I got it. It's mine. There's more. Don't worry."

She looked at the check. She looked at the ducks. She looked at me.

I said, "It's your way out."

She tried to hand it back to me and I put my hands up so she couldn't.

"You always said you wanted to get out," I said.

"But—I—I don't know how."

"Call me when you get where you're going and I can help you figure it out. Maybe we can meet out west like you always wanted. Right? Wouldn't that be cool? Just don't tell anyone. It's a cashier's check. It's like cash. I don't want them taking it from you."

"I—uh..."

She put the check in her skirt pocket. She pressed on it to make sure it was there. I did too. Then I hugged her and went back across the road because I heard a car coming.

Then, there it was, exactly as my transmission had shown me. Ellie stood in the field by herself, crying, surrounded by her ducks. The car pulled up. She stepped into it and they drove away. She didn't look back.

I watched and my heart broke.

It broke because I knew the transmissions were true.

It broke because I knew what was coming. For Ellie. For me. For the world.

———

"We have to get a real oven," I said to Dad. "We can't keep eating this microwaved shit."

He looked at me over his glasses.

"Electric," I said.

He nodded.

"You okay?" I asked.

"I ordered canvas last night, you'll be happy to know."

I smiled.

"I'm going to paint the ovens," he said. "I can see them." He tapped his skull. "I can see them in here."

We will be surrounded by ovens. We will be gluttons after years of starvation. Ovens will be our outlet. He will paint. I will cook.

And we will have a future.

———

I called Peter that night from Darla's rocking chair on the front porch. I didn't flirt. I just told him I wanted to talk more about psychology. I told him I was interested in college.

"Will you be at the mall tomorrow?" he asked. "We can talk about it over lunch."

"How about you move your experiment to Main Street? Plenty of passersby," I said. "Half the restaurants have outside tables, too. We could sit all day and smile at people."

"True," he said. "See you there. Noon. That Irish pub place."

When I hung up, my train—the one that had been speeding down the track for a week—came to a graceful stop. No one in the passenger car was jarred. No food spilled in the dining car. The sleepers in the sleeping cars weren't in any way inconvenienced.

It just stopped. And I got off. It was the beginning of the history of the future and it was the end of Max Black.

And I would live.

Glory O'Brien's History of the Future

There will be spaceships. There will be cures for every disease including hatred. We will knock the chips off our shoulders. We will realize, as the population of the galaxy reaches the hundred trillions, that we are no one special. We will realize that all of us are here to do something. Our job is to find out what that is. And all will be equal—plumbers, presidents, movie stars, ditchdiggers—and no one will want to just sit and waste time. Because life will be short again.

The cosmic palindrome will whittle us down to elderly fifty-year-olds. To creatures with life spans like pets on Earth in the twenty-first century—every moment with them treasured.

Yet, we will be mundane.

Yet, we will be no one special.

It will not be about who we think we are. It will be about what we do.

I will do great things.

You will do great things.

Most people can't handle that.

Can you?

Acknowledgments

To write books is a solitary thing. To put a book in a reader's hand is most certainly *not* a solitary thing. Thank you to my agent, Michael Bourret; to my editor, Andrea Spooner; and to Deirdre Jones, Victoria Stapleton, and the entire team at LBYR.

Librarians, teachers, booksellers, and bloggers, I cannot thank you enough for your support. Without you, where would I be? Not here, I tell you. Not here. If I could send you all a herd of goats or a home-baked pie in return for what you do, I would. For now, please accept .my gratitude and a hug the next time I see you. Unless you don't like hugs. Then I will high-five, nod, or wave.

Andrew Smith kept me sane as I wrote and edited this book. It should be duly noted that he is not only a genius writer but also a great friend and a top-notch golfer. Also, thank you to the students of Bryan High School in Omaha who heard the first pages of this book in December 2011 and told me to finish it so they could find out the rest of the story. You all taught me so much that week. You know what I'm talking about. Stay real. It's the only way to wade through the bullshit.

I realize I have used an eight-letter *F* word in this book that some may not like. (Hint: It ends with *eminist*.) I want to thank my parents for raising me with that *F* word and for not succumbing to the consumerist pink nonsense that was shoved toward them from every direction as they raised three daughters. Be proud, Sarigs. You are the history of our future.

To Topher and my girls, who put up with the life of this author: I love you. I couldn't do this without your support and understanding. Thank you. I can't think of three other people I'd rather form, shine, and burn with. Kapow.